Come Back Irish

Come Back Irish

Wendy Rawlings

WINNER OF THE
SANDSTONE PRIZE
IN SHORT FICTION

The Ohio State University Press
Columbus

Library of Congress Cataloging-in-Publication Data

Rawlings, Wendy.
    Come back Irish / Wendy Rawlings.
        p. cm.
"Winner of the Sandstone prize in short fiction."
    ISBN 0-8142-0887-8 (cloth : alk. paper) —
    ISBN 0-8142-5085-8 (pbk. : alk. paper)
1. Ireland—Social life and customs—Fiction.
2. Americans—Ireland—Fiction. I. Title.
    PS3618.R39 C66 2001
    813'.6—dc21

                                    2001001551

Text and cover design by Paula Newcomb.
Type set in ITC Berkeley Old Style by Sans Serif Inc.
Printed by McNaughton & Gunn.

The paper used in this publication meets the
minimum requirements of the American National
Standard for Information Sciences—Permanence of
Paper for Printed Library Materials.
ANSI Z39.48-1992.

9   8   7   6   5   4   3   2   1

Acknowledgments

I am grateful to The MacDowell Colony, The Virginia Center for the Creative Arts, and the Corporation of Yaddo, under whose roofs several of these stories were written.

I wish to thank those that published these stories, sometimes in different form: *The Atlantic Monthly, The Chattahoochee Review, Cimarron Review, Colorado Review, New Letters, Prism International,* and *Western Humanities Review.* For their help along the way, I am indebted to Meg Brady, Karen Brennan, C. Michael Curtis, Emily Hammond, Steven Schwartz, and W3: Kristen Gould-Case, Heather Hirschi, Dawn Marano, Susan Sample, Dorothy Solomon, and Kate Woodworth.

My gratitude to my parents and sister—Gayle, David, and Darcy—for their interest and support. A special thanks to Declan for the ten and two.

For Chris Robertson,
most constant friend

Contents

Come Back Irish

Beth was going to learn Irish. She had gotten herself a slim illustrated book called *Speak Irish Now*. There were pictures of kitchen implements, body parts, a hurley stick, sheep. But the words on the page were a traffic jam of consonants, indigestible as bricks. For instance, *d'fhanfadh*. For instance, *ndeachaigh*. Most of the words seemed to be about the same length. They were cunningly unphonetic; they got shipwrecked in her windpipe. They were, as a woman from Killibegs had once told her about her countrymen, a clannish lot.

After six years on Long Island, Beth had begun hassling Eamon about going home with him. No time, he had said, no money. Then his father had unexpectedly bounced back from a pair of heart attacks: a sign, Eamon said, that he should spend his savings on tickets home.

At JFK lightning storms delayed their flight. Eamon found a kiosk that sold only Murphy's and traded two five-dollar bills for flimsy plastic cups of stout. He held his cup high in the air.

"You're a great woman, so you are," he told Beth. "It'll be grand, you and my dad in McCormack's for big filthy pints. For that alone he'll want to marry you."

His sisters only drank the crème de menthes. It was the German beer for his brothers, lager after lager. His mother had been a devoted whiskey drinker when she was alive, a noggin of Jameson's she finished each night, then filled with tea and milk for Eamon to take to school. "I was the only one who thought she drank the whole bottle so I could have something to hold my tea in the morning," he said.

A zigzag of lightning cracked against the sky. Beth jumped.

"What you need," Eamon said, "is a Guinness and black currant. For the nerves."

Beth was drawn to brogues, Emerald Isle kitsch, the shillelagh-and-tea-cloth brand of Irishness. Now she had a match game of family member and favorite drink to help keep track of all the relatives, a kind of mnemonic device in a glass. She would even have one for herself: a rich dark stew of stout and syrup.

When at last their plane taxied down the runway and took off, the flight became an airborne booze cruise, the passengers' demands for little bottles of liquor noisy and unabated. Beth took out *Speak Irish Now* and read while she drank her little bottle of Chardonnay. Foreign-language primers always seemed inordinately preoccupied with the weather.

"I think it's *flichshneachta* out there," she said.

What was that, Eamon asked.

"Sleet."

"You'll get a lot of *flichshneachta* in Ireland," he said. He explained Beth's interest in the Irish language to the passenger beside them, an ancient man with a throaty, incomprehensible Cork brogue and a carpeting of dandruff across the shoulders of his suit jacket.

"No one has Irish anymore," the man said fiercely. He might have been objecting to shoes of a certain era, an outdated dance step. He ceremoniously offered Beth a throat lozenge, then joined Eamon in pretending they needed Beth to order extra cans of beer for them.

When they stood to deplane in Dublin, the man offered Beth

one cold hand. "*Ní thabharfadh an duine sin deoch uisce duit,*" he said, then vanished.

"What did he say?" Beth whispered.

"He said you wouldn't give a man a drink of water."

❖ ❖ ❖

At customs they had to separate; Eamon and his Irish passport with a gold harp printed on the cover went to the left, Beth and her eagle-embossed one to the right. He walked backwards and waved to her as he got in line with the other Irish citizens—a young mother with a yowling baby and three stooped old men. Eamon looked oversized among them, a giant boy in a white sweatshirt scarred brown down the front with stout.

Yet even Eamon was, after a decade in America, adulterated, only a partial Irishman, an uncomfortable Hibernian hybrid. "Resident alien," the card in his wallet declared him, like some half-recognizable species—a turnip with a human head. He had always wanted to live here, he often said as they drove in heavy traffic toward Manhattan's show-off of a skyline, but he had always wanted to stay back home. "My detoured leprechaun," Beth told him, stroking the predictable cleft in his chin. "Cleft-chinned smithy of my soul."

But here they were, in the real Ireland, beyond the litter of claddagh rings and Erin go bragh, the high-stepping of River-dance on videocassette. Beth joined the long line for citizens of other countries, mostly Americans. Members of an elderly tour group were loudly exchanging greetings: "Top o' the morning to ye." The customs agents in their booths looked upon everyone, Beth thought, with unchanging expressions of glum suspicion. Maybe they didn't like such smarmy American aping of Irishness. Eamon himself hated Saint Patrick's Day, with its green-beered drunkenness and plastic bowler hats. Once she had gotten him a card with a shamrock on it, and he'd laughed, but it hadn't been the laugh she'd wanted.

They would be staying at Eamon's father's house, the only place unpopulated by the brood of children his brothers and sisters had produced. Beth wished for a bed-and-breakfast, someplace tidy and uninhabited by decay. She pictured Eamon's father as a skeleton propped up in a corner, a death mask haunting a chair. Her own grandfather had recently died after years suspended in dementia, as if in some viscous, clotty fluid. At the end he had thought he was conductor on the Long Island Rail Road, and then a baby who couldn't get enough to eat. Beth had held his head up while her mother spooned strained bananas into his mouth, the two of them cooing at him in the language of babies, all vowels. It was the closest she'd ever felt to her grandfather, the sticky syllables of the language falling away, stripped of its consonants. Hadn't she once hoped she and Eamon might find, in the sweaty wordless aftermath of sex, a place like this, where language was no longer even necessary?

On this trip Beth would translate herself like a language, make of herself something as legible as block letters. She grinned at the customs official when she handed him her passport, and was disappointed when he didn't bother to wink or tell her to enjoy her stay in Ireland. Near the baggage carousel she found Eamon squatting on their suitcases and smoking a cigarette. "John Joe must've had a desperate head on him this morning," he said, then held up the keys for the car he'd rented. "We're on our own."

Driving to Eamon's hometown, Beth fretted. She clipped and unclipped the barrette in her hair, put on lipstick and then rubbed it off with a napkin, needled Eamon with questions. How Catholic was his family? Would it matter that they weren't married? Would they disapprove of her?

"For feck's sake, Beth," he said. He pointed to the green-and-yellow checkerboard flags flying in front of all the houses. They had entered his county. The All-Ireland Gaelic football final was coming up, he told her. No one would care if she were a one-legged Buddhist. Beth had noticed a lot of talk about Gaelic football in *Speak Irish Now*, much of it accompanied by cartoons depicting disgruntled spectators in striped jerseys. *"Ní bhuafaidh siad sín cluiche go deo,"* one character said to another. *They'll never win a match.*

She had thought the scenery—cows blinking slowly in their pastures, the hills in their patchworked forty shades of green—would calm her, but Eamon whipped so quickly around turns that her body set up a lurching metronomic rhythm. Finally she saw a crumbling stone castle and a small shop with a sign that read, PAWS-A-WHILE. Outside Paws-A-While someone had hung a handmade sign that said, SALE MANURE.

"We'll go see Paddy first." Eamon swung the car into a development signposted Avondale Estate. The word *estate* flooded her with a sense of largesse. As a child she had boarded a pony in a small barn behind her house. One afternoon she had, in a moment of pure misunderstanding of her own motives, encouraged it to bite her. The pony did not seriously injure her, but not long afterward her mother had sold it to the parents of a boy about her age. The stable had never been used again, except for trysts with boyfriends and a few unfortunate incidents with schnapps.

She peered out at the squat gray two-story apartment buildings, rows upon rows of attached housing. Someone had draped all the hedges with green-and-yellow plastic banners. Checkerboard flags fluttered outside every apartment. A two-page color photo of the football team from the newspaper had been pasted on several windowpanes. "UP MEATH" was scrawled in the dirt on the back of some parked cars, "BOO MAYO" on others. From a second-story window a Meath jersey twisted on a hanger in the breeze.

"Jaysus, the atmosphere is great," Eamon said.

From the center of one yard a large bush shaped like a lopsided person waved, a flag jutting from a leafy fist. A green-and-yellow cap had been placed on top of the bush at a jaunty angle.

"Jaysus, that's great," he said again. He kept shaking his head and smiling. Beth found herself possessed by a wish, for the first time in several years of courtship, to tell him to shut up. He suddenly seemed to her parochial and quaint, whereas in all the time she had known him he had seemed charming and quaint. The sculpted bush was dumb. She felt embarrassed for the people with the jersey hanging in their window.

They found Paddy watching television and eating tiny squares of cheese and tomato sandwiches off a cutting board on his lap. "Beth, is it?" he asked, then hugged her and said she was lovely for a Yank. Tea and cigarettes and sandwiches were offered all around, the sandwiches so covered with pepper that Beth's mouth felt sandy. It unnerved her that Eamon called his father by his first name.

❖ ❖ ❖

After a day or so the jet lag receded, but Beth still felt soiled and disoriented. There did not seem to be any proper heat source in Paddy's house. The showerhead produced only a forlorn trickle. On the third morning she woke early and decided to make the tea. A lacy string of cobwebs stood between her and the inside of the china cabinet, where she could see a stack of teacups and a bottle of green dish detergent labeled Fairy Liquid.

She was trying to decide whether to put her hand through the cobwebs when Paddy joined her. He was a small, trim, vigorous man, despite a persistent wheeze that often escalated into fits of coughing. Eamon's sisters had spoken as if he were winding down toward his last days, but he looked deceptively bright with life for someone who had suffered a pair of heart attacks. "You don't smoke," he said, holding out his pack of cigarettes nonetheless, as if Beth might suddenly change her mind. "Do you take a drink?"

"Oh, yes," she said. "I like a Guinness."

This seemed to cheer him considerably. "A lovely pint of Guinness, with a creamy head," he said. Now hungry, apparently, he took an unlabeled glass jar from the refrigerator and began to feed hurriedly on its contents. Beth smelled vinegar.

At lunch, which he called dinner, he peeled potatoes into Beth's bowl with his hands, making a pile of brown jackets on a saucer in the center of the table. When he was a boy, he said, everyone squatted in the middle of the floor and ate their potatoes out of the same big bowl.

"The bollocks is making things up again," Eamon said.

Once, at an Irish pub in Manhattan on Saint Patrick's Day, three Irishmen who claimed to be security guards at a tampon factory in Hoboken had bought Beth drinks. Late in the evening, drunk, she had come out of the bathroom and heard them speaking to each other in a flat, nasal accent that she immediately recognized as an imitation of her own. In that moment she had hated them, for their in-jokes, their unwavering nationalism, their milk-white skin and unabashed poverty, their habit of talking over and across her in Irish, a language no one else knew or cared to know.

"Do you believe in the hereafter?" Paddy asked.

Beth saw she had plowed through all the potatoes he had given her. "I don't know," she said.

"Eamon says you're Jewish."

"Not really."

"What's that? Were you not born Jewish?"

"I was just born," Beth said.

He offered her his jar of pickled onions. Three still lolled in the bottom, submerged in murky vinegar like tiny preserved heads. "Try them," he said, beaming at her. "They're lovely." With one hand he traced the route from his throat to his stomach. "Next time I'll come back as a pint and go to a good home."

"Next time I want to come back Irish," Beth said. She wanted to be a citizen of a country with its own enviably embarrassing cultural identity (the cheerful, capering drunk), its own universally recognized songs and symbols and history ("Danny Boy," shamrock, Famine), its own unpronounceable language cluttered with consonants. She pointed to the only nouns in the room she could remember. "*Cupan. Taephota.*"

Paddy winked at her. "*Níl me ag caint Gaelige.*"

"You must have learned it in school."

"Sure, now, we were too busy fighting the Norsemen in those days to waste our time with the likes of school." He winked, shrugged, peeled more potatoes into her bowl.

❖❖❖

Later, at the Haggard Inn and then in the lounge of the Judge and Jury, Beth was persuaded to do a Jewish accent. She imitated her mother haranguing a white-coated saleswoman at the Clinique counter in Bloomingdale's. "In the past few years my poas have gotten very large. Do you have something for large poas?" Then her parents arguing over a bad investment her father had made in someone's nephew's foray into frozen pizza rolls. Then her father complaining about his sciatica. Most of this Beth invented as she went. Her parents were mild, box-of-matzo-in-the-cabinet Jews, their income modest by Long Island standards. Still, Eamon's family fanned out on either side of her, roaring. Eamon roared.

"But they don't really talk like that, sure they don't?" his sister Siobhan said.

"Sure they do." Siobhan's husband, John Joe, rested an elbow on a large fold of belly. He had an ulcer and kept singing "Desiree," not the whole song but just the word. "Remember that show *Rhoda*?"

Everyone agreed that Beth sounded like Rhoda. Proof from television seemed to settle the matter. In America, association with television seemed to discredit facts, but in Ireland television seemed to stand as that which validated all claims.

"You should see the house where Beth grew up," Eamon was saying. "Like the mansion on *Dynasty*."

"Is it really?" Siobhan asked.

"That would be a gross exaggeration," Beth said primly, but nobody heard her. Eamon was describing the maid's quarters, the stables, the billiards room with the full bar, the ice machine, the monogrammed highball glasses.

"But there's nothing in the stables," Beth insisted. "The stables are falling down."

Now they looked at Beth differently: inhabitant of mansions, owner of highball glasses. She had meant to distance herself from that, to align with Eamon; but now she felt herself to be a species apart from him and his family, with their forlorn and graying teeth, their tiny identical row houses, the Waterford crystal from their weddings everywhere locked up and dusty, their unself-conscious public singing. Two young men with fiddles had wandered into the pub and began to play. People sang along between swigs of stout, mispronouncing most of the words. They said "tree," for instance, when they meant "three." She wondered if she should drink more.

She drank, the stout a brogue's lubricant. It made her recoil from the sound of her American accent reverberating inside her head—the nasal monotony of it, the apathetic blah blah blah of someone middle-class, cushioned by the class below her, someone raised by a mother who had time to worry about pores, someone who could indulge a whim and get bitten by ponies and drunk on melonberry schnapps. She had no tragic history to recall, only a road back through memory filled with the discarded gifts and purchases of an American childhood.

John Joe was telling a story about going out for Chinese food with a crowd in Navan. The taxi driver who took them home had gotten paid twice, by him and then by Siobhan.

"Eejits," Siobhan said, as if she were commenting on the behavior of some other drunk and foolish couple.

"Drink up, lads," the bartenders were calling.

Though it was after midnight, the streets were busy with people walking home from the pubs, arm in arm or in unruly shouting clusters. Eamon draped one arm around Beth's neck, leaning heavily on her. They passed a butcher shop. The scarlet sides of meat hanging in the window affronted Beth. She had wanted to ask Eamon about the shops he had gone to as a child, the architecture of the Christian Brothers school, the fields where he'd played Gaelic football. There was a statue of some English lord up by the hotel she'd meant to ask about—an early colonizer?

"Oh, that," Eamon said. "They've been trying to blow that up for years." He gestured toward his family, walking on ahead in the joyous and disorganized zigzag of drunks and children. "We never get around to anything."

"You didn't have to say that about *Dynasty*," Beth said.

"They liked your accent. They liked 'poas.'"

"They liked 'poas,'" Beth said. "Great." She felt glum and violated, like a bed someone had pissed by accident.

They went back to Siobhan and John Joe's house, a messier twin of Paddy's. John Joe, complaining of his ulcer, lay on the couch and drank milk from the carton. He was still singing "Desiree." Siobhan clopped from one room to another, shouting at everyone to keep it down or the girls would wake up. The girls woke up and wandered in, barefooted and squinting, tangles in their hair. They nodded when Siobhan introduced them and had to be told to shake hands with Beth. The taller one, Nuala, prodded John Joe with a foot. "Drunk again?" she asked. "Did you go to McCormack's? Have you a packet of crisps for me?"

The girls showed Beth their room. It seemed to be a converted storage area, with flimsy walls they had written on in pencil. More UP MEATH. More BOO MAYO. "If Meath win, everyone gets the day off from school, but if Mayo win, we don't get the day off but the boys' school does," said Nuala. The younger girl, Ciara, sucked her thumb and asked Beth if she could touch her hair.

"You're drunk, too," Nuala said.

"You look like your father," said Beth.

"But not fat."

"And not drunk," said Beth.

❖❖❖

That night, the Guinness and black currant made her hallucinate. She saw the world in triplicate, three turning orbs. Three of herself bought scarlet sides of beef in the butcher shop from a man without a tongue. At the top of a staircase she stood in mink, white diamonds dripping from her breasts like milk. The man on the plane with the dandruff-covered shoulders grabbed her and cackled sour syllables into her mouth.

She felt a presence next to her, an arm slung around her waist. She got out of bed. The long tiled hallway felt as slick as a frozen pond under her feet. When she finished peeing, she flushed the handle while still sitting on the bowl and felt air whoosh up between her thighs. The ancient plumbing chortled as the water went down. She crossed back to the room where she and Eamon slept and climbed in beside him. He slept sprawled out when he drank, a limb in each direction. She pushed the cold soles of her feet against his legs. He yelped helplessly and turned on his side.

"Do you still love me?" she whispered to his shoulder blade. The Guinness had receded, leaving her head trapped in an aching, sugary halo. She remembered the cartoons of men with sore heads, each one holding his pint of the black stuff. Language primers also liked illness. A headache was *tinneas cinn*. Was *cinn* pronounced like sin?

"Get some sleep, Beth." He reached for her hand and held it hard against his hip.

In the morning she found Eamon and Paddy downing tea in the living room. "It's herself!" Paddy announced. Eamon wore the green-and-yellow cap that had been on the bush in the yard. He tossed her a Meath jersey.

"I'm not wearing this." She threw it back at him and went to put on her own clothes.

"You'll look like an eejit in cashmere," he warned.

She had not showered in two days—a record for her. She

sniffed her armpits. They smelled like the microwaved kasha she'd gotten on the plane. She felt as if she were soggy grain, fermenting.

❖ ❖ ❖

Dublin bustled with pregame drunkenness, everyone spilling out of the pubs in their green-and-yellow jerseys. "This is a Meath pub," Eamon said as he elbowed his way in. People rebounded off Beth, flecking her sweater with spots of stout. After drinking two pints of Guinness, she let Eamon help her pull the Meath jersey on over her sweater. "You look lovely," he said, and kissed her, stuffing his tongue in her mouth.

She trotted along behind him to the stadium. Their tickets were for an area called Hill Sixteen—a section with no seats, only low cement walls to lean on. "What if we get trampled?" she shouted, but the cheering and roaring drowned her out. Mary Robinson came out dressed in purple silk, and everyone stood for the national anthem. They sang in Irish, loose lilting syllables that Beth couldn't form. She still often made the mistake of walking into the men's room, labeled FIR. Women's was MNA, which she always transposed into MAN.

Eamon shouted all through the match. Beth had trouble keeping track of the ball, which got not just kicked but also dribbled and thrown. It was like watching basketball and soccer and football all at the same time. Meath pulled ahead by a point in the last two minutes of the match. "Brilliant," Eamon breathed. His eyes glinted with tears. In front of them two men with pom-poms on their hats threw themselves into the crowds below. Eamon was hugging the man beside him and weeping.

"Jesus, Eamon. Pull yourself together." Beth patted him on the back. It was the first time she had seen him weep. It made her want to drink.

They rode home with Siobhan and John Joe. The tradition, apparently, was to stop at pubs along the homeward route. A replay was being held in every little hamlet, each moment of the game worked over in murderous detail. "Sure they won, but they played crap," Siobhan said.

The Guinness was blurring the edges of things. Beth was starting to like life better this way—everything bleeding together. "They played crap," she agreed.

From under a straw hat that seemed to be gradually unraveling on her head, Siobhan offered her a wavering, contentious look.

Beth had been practicing her accent, the way she practiced Irish words and "poas." Usually she practiced in her head. But something had unhooked in her. A bolus of four consonants pushed together stuck in her throat, a halitosis of want, for after all she wasn't, would never be, Irish. "I didn't mean it like that," she said.

"Go get a round from the barman." Eamon pushed a roll of banknotes into her hand.

While she was up at the bar, a singing began—first in scattered clusters, then a chorus, then a ragged harmony. The crowd, surging up for drinks, pinned her against the bar. In the corner Siobhan put one arm around John Joe and the other around Eamon. A man with an accordion climbed up on a table and began to play with restless, fanatic energy. He lay down on his back, still playing, and gulped a pint of Guinness poured into his mouth from above.

❖ ❖ ❖

Over the next few weeks things began moving more and more slowly, as if drifting in the Liffey, rife with pollutants. Each night Beth and Eamon went with Paddy to Siobhan and John Joe's for a meal, usually dark brown and stewed. Afterward they lingered for hours at the table with multiple cups of tea, any uneaten food congealing on the plates in front of them. Beth became convinced that the nightly pints of Guinness, opaque and dense as oak, had gone solid in her body, her organs shellacked. Her limbs stiffened; she had to mind them when she walked through doorways. Her Irish wasn't coming along as she'd expected. People spoke it in jest and secret, muttered quickly, like drug transactions she'd seen on the Lower East Side of Manhattan. The words slid out of the sides of mouths, meant for other ears.

It should be noted that the English language is weighted toward action, control, independence, she read in her primer.

"I am happy."
"I am sad."

In contrast, the Irish language explicitly recognizes distinctions between action and patience.

táim go bronach	"I exist sadly."
tá bron orm	"Sadness exists on me."

A stubborn clump of rain clouds gathered over Eamon's town and stayed as if pasted there. It rained gray sheets for days. The weather began dueling with the Gaelic football win as a topic of conversation, but no one seemed daunted by all the *flichshneachta*: women walked out for their groceries in it with little more cover than rain hats; children tumbled on the greens with their soccer balls, oblivious even of downpours. Beth thought about sadness existing on her, a beige miasma, a misty blight. She felt her soul, assailed, soaked through, retreating into its crawl space. The peat Paddy brought in to burn in the fireplace steamed when he lit it. Even the food acquired a musty taste, musty cheese on stiff bread, flat Lucozade that Eamon and Paddy never capped tightly enough, so that it lost its fizz and tasted to Beth like glucose solution.

At night she huddled in bed and warmed her hands on Eamon's shoulders, a Girl Scout tending a tiny fire. "We can't stay here much longer," she said. "Rent is due back home in a week."

"We can wire it from here."

Outside, rain clacked against the windows. In the past few

days the hills around the town had gone deep and then deeper green, a hegemony of green.

"I want to go home," she whispered. "Do you want to stay?"

They lay for a long time like that, her hands at his back. Then he got up and left the room, returning with a carton of milk. He gulped from it and handed it to her. It had started to sour, the first inkling of curdle.

"It's gone off," she said, gagging a little as some of it slipped down her throat.

He took the carton from her and lay back on his side of the bed. She heard the milk slosh into his mouth, a dumb sour ocean between them.

"Then stay," he said. "Then go."

Heteroworld

You thought everyone got off at that exit, your parents and their parents and everyone's parents paired Noah's ark-like, ready to set out to sea in the ribs of their own small ships, freighted down with all the appliances they asked for: espresso maker, bread baker, candlesticks pewter, place mats gray. Those first weeks, the two of them swathed at night in the bedroom colors your mother chose at Macy's, slate and granite, their marriage bed a stone quarry of colors. Together they got drunk, got pregnant, got married, got a set of towels, got a Jack Russell terrier they finally agreed, after arguments about Cuddles or Bart, to name Jack Russell. They'd have a girl he'd name, a girl she'd name, an argument about what to do with a wealthy uncle's name they were supposed to give a boy that your father wanted to try for and your mother didn't.

You have a blurry memory of watching your mother breastfeed your sister on the beanbag chair in the living room, the purply afghan she knitted thrown over her knees, the new nameless baby gorging on her while she shouted to your father, cooking chicken curry in the next room, "Michelle? Maura? Melissa?" Your mother wanted an "M" name, after her grandparents Miriam and Max, both dead of heart attacks that same year, 1972. Your grandmother was lobbying for Mindy, a name your mother vetoed, but the one your grandmother called your sister all her life. This was the same grandmother who decided your name should have been Clarina. To you this still sounds like a cleaning agent, the caustic blue of chlorine, disinfecting the pisses your boy cousins took in your grandparents' pool.

Luckily, your mother was on a Barbara Stanwyck kick when she had you, luckily (she often had to remind your grandmother), the first place you took up residence was her, not your grandmother, who is now in Palm Beach forgetting everything, Clarina and Mindy, Babs and Molly, the arc of her life erasing messily, like a mark on a sheet of paper under that Holly Hobbie eraser you kept on the end of your pencil for show even though it ripped a hole in the paper every time you used it.

You paraphrase to yourself what your mother tells you long-distance from Long Island: your grandmother is being Holly Hobbied right out of her mind, Alzheimered into oblivion. When she dies two years from now, completely unaware of who you are or who she was, she will leave you not savings bonds but two identical sets of jewelry, one in a music box that smells faintly of disinfectant, the other, the real stuff, which will look as if she never actually wore it, in a safety deposit box in the bank. She will die never knowing that your mother, in the middle of menopause, divorced your father and got, so to speak, back on the highway.

Homoland. For you this exit has been, you admit, perpetually Under Construction, like summer roadwork on the Long Island Expressway. If people got off there it was surreptitiously and at their own risk, kicking up dust and neon orange pylons as they rode up on the shoulder. You had never driven onto this exit's service road, had only glimpsed it from Heteroworld's broad highway. You had, for instance, seen *La Cage aux Folles*. You had paused on Christopher Street to peer through the darkened windows of the taverns with rainbow flags hanging above the entrances. Once you had flown to Dublin beside a man from Carbondale in a yellow silk jacket who stayed on the mattress beside you at the youth hostel in Dame Street and invited you to tag along when he went out to the pubs, which turned out to be Hooray Harry's, Abba's "Dancing Queen" pulsing at you from all sides, making your viscera ache. Abba was all that was pulsing at you. You had never seen so many red-headed gay men with brogues.

That was it: Homoland as Vacationland, a dizzying Disney World of drag queening and dyke biking. You had never been far enough off the exit ramp to find your way into the suburbs, where gay couples keep herb gardens and chlorinate their pools and argue in Pathmark about whether to get a case of Miller Lite or go all out and get the Corona and limes. But there's your mother teaching herself how to dry flowers and tie them with ribbon so she can hang them over the bathroom mirror in the tiny rented cottage where she lives now; there's Ursula cleaning leaves out of the roof gutters on a ladder in the front yard. A year ago you were the daughter of a nice middle-class couple. Now you're an honorary member of the Rainbow Coalition, your mother proclaiming this with stickers on the rear windshield of the used BMW your father bought from his boss for her fiftieth birthday.

Ten miles away, your father is booking a trip to Saint Thomas with his new girlfriend, a music therapist who has just crawled out of Heteroworld's bad neighborhood, the rogue's gallery of black eyes and drunken Sundays, her ex-husband cruising the street where she lives with a shotgun in the backseat of his truck. You're glad she met your dad, who splints the broken bones of injured animals and does yoga and alternate nostril breathing before sunrise each morning. When you take your summer holidays and your dad asks if you mind if his new girl-friend comes to the airport with him to pick you up, you thank the first deity that comes to mind that she is plain and middle-aged and, yes, small-breasted. On the way home in the car she plays Joni Mitchell for you on her guitar while you sprawl in the backseat and drink beers out of the mini cooler your dad has brought for you. You have never been much of a Joni Mitchell fan, but in this moment you are thrilled about Joni Mitchell, who is a little maimed by childhood polio and hippie-imperfect like this woman in the front seat—not a blonde bombshell, not a supermodel, not an adolescent.

"I'm just glad he chose a *woman*," your sister had said. Poor Molly, a sophomore at Duke, recent pledge of Kappa Kappa Gamma, phoned at two o'clock in the morning to tell you she'd been plucked from among the ordinary like the fleur-de-lis that was the symbol of her new sisterhood. She had already learned a sorority song, "Sisters Bonded," which she sang, slightly off-key and, you suspected, a little drunkenly, for she was slurring and had mentioned tequila slammers. "I'm so happy for my baby sister," you said into the phone, though during your own college days you bowed out halfway through the first week of sorority rush, unable to smile that hard without your face falling apart. Instead you headed back to your dog-eared Dostoyevsky, Dickens, Flaubert, Tolstoy, where you wandered jealously through the pages of that fraternity, not knowing that George Eliot was one of your own.

Molly is bonding with her forty-four sisters over Diet Cokes or Miller Lites in the Rathskeller, your mother's secret folded up in the back of her throat like sore tonsils. Your mother's secret is caught and aching in the back of her throat at the sorority formal amid the blur of smiling for photographers and dancing boozily to James Brown and drinking cranberry vodkas and puking cranberry vodkas and sleeping with a fraternity brother at the Sigma Nu house and getting a pregnancy test and getting birth control pills and worrying about AIDS and not doing anything about AIDS and listening to the Sigma Nu brothers make jokes about AIDS and jokes about homos and still Molly is not saying anything about your mother, who is living a quiet and entirely conventional life except for one small detail in a beach community on the north shore of Long Island.

Your father drops you off at the cottage your mother rents

with Ursula and tells you to call him on Sunday night. You're going out to Montauk for the weekend with your mother and Ursula and their friends Kate and Liz and Stephanie and Martha. You'll be the only heterosexual in the crowd, the token straight girl. "Martha" has always seemed like a straight-girl name to you, so you're surprised to meet a Martha who shakes your hand briskly and goes crashing into the ocean in a Rangers tee shirt and cutoffs. At cocktail hour your mother and Ursula serve champagne in plastic glasses and everyone toasts everyone and you drink too much too fast and go for a swim to clear your head. You let yourself get knocked under by a wave, your legs scraped raw in the sand. Every summer in your childhood you vacationed out here, you and Molly sharing the pull-out sofa beside your parents' bed at the White Sands Motel. The sheets were always damp with sea air, and Molly sometimes pissed the bed in the night, the two of you waking in the morning sweaty and intertwined and stinking a little of pee.

Luckily, you're staying at a different motel, the Wavecrest, but your mother and Ursula have had to cut corners to afford this holiday. The three of you are sharing a room with Stephanie and Martha, lawyers who don't have to cut corners—who are letting the three of you, in fact, hang out in theirs. Ursula insists that you sleep on the pull-out sofa with your mother. She inflates an air mattress on the floor and settles in with a detective novel.

Once, early in their relationship, before you even really knew what was going on between them, you and your mother and Ursula were having steamers and Chardonnay and your mother started in on you about your boyfriend. He was treating you badly, he was Irish and weren't most of them alcoholic? Was he even legal in this country and why take up with someone divorced with a child anyway? You had gotten up and cleared your plate, the empty clam shells knocked into the garbage on top of the remains of your mother's NutriSystem freeze-dried lasagna lunch, and then you headed off to your own room, and the mistake Ursula had made was following you. Some lesbian folksinger on the tape deck and your mother crying in her wine and Ursula in your doorway telling you this advice was for your own good, they just didn't want you to get hurt, that was all, and you looked at her and said, *I don't know what you are, but you're not my mother and you're not her spokesperson.*

You know Ursula and your mother are working hard not to freak you out; some of your best friends are gay, but this is your mother after all, your mother who looked so much like Natalie Wood when you were little that people used to stop her on the street and tell her so, your mother who at Paul D. Schreiber High School was not just a cheerleader but voted homecoming queen and "most popular" and "best teeth." In her high school yearbook your father, bookish in thick glasses, the actor who played Tom Wingfield in his senior year production of *The Glass Menagerie,* wrote next to his picture that he hoped your mother would find "the appreciating mate she deserved."

You lie in bed beside your mother and listen to the sounds of everyone dropping off to sleep, Stephanie and Martha and your mother and then Ursula, snoring noisily on the floor below you. From the Atlantic the sea air drifts in, and in your dream your sister is five and beside you, curled up against your hip.

❖ ❖ ❖

Your parents divorced "amicably," as they say, which is why you end up, on the last day of your vacation, drinking premixed margaritas late in the afternoon on an old comforter at Jones Beach with them. They're not married anymore but that doesn't mean they're not your parents, they tell you. From a beach vendor selling Guatemalan jewelry your parents buy you a pair of earrings, dangly and beset with blood-colored beads. You go for a swim with your father, the sea choppy with froth, him shouting "over" when the waves are small enough and "under" when they're colossal and folding over on top of you, the way he taught you not to drown when you were six. You can see your mother sitting by herself on the shore, one hand shading her eyes while she watches you. She was never a strong swimmer, always worried you and Molly would get dragged out to sea. Once, the two of you did get pulled out by the undertow, and you watched your mother running toward you as she yanked her flowered sundress over her head and waded helplessly in her bikini into the breakwater, shouting that she was coming for you, don't panic, she would save you. Some college boys playing Frisbee heard her and swam out and brought the two of you back to her, and you stood bleating like newborns while she blotted and wrapped you in a towel.

Your father still calls your mother "Binky," the nickname her grandfather gave her one Hanukkah in the early fifties when he gave her a Binky doll from F.A.O. Schwartz that looked just like her, the eyes the skin the glossy hair, even the shape of the features, remarkable the resemblance. She used to carry the doll under her arm always, a second self.

You and your parents drive home from the beach in your father's company car, Joni Mitchell warbling on the tape deck. You might in this moment hate Joni Mitchell a little. In the backseat you drift off, the Wantaugh Parkway to the Northern State Parkway to Route 25-A a familiar lull in your limbs. You must have gone this route hundreds, thousands of times, one parent or the other navigating in one car or another: the green Volkswagen with the apple painted on the driver's side door, the red Chevy Impala with the peeling black upholstery that burned your legs in summer, the blue Valiant with the hole in the floor where you and Molly looked through and watched the road blur by.

Your father drops you and your mother off, and you kiss him good-bye and your mother doesn't.

"Bye, Binks," he says, and then he's gone.

❖❖❖

On Christmas Eve, Molly arrives in an ivory pantsuit and takes you out for spiked eggnog. She can't deal with it, she says into her drink, doesn't want a lesbian for a mother, doesn't want a caricature, a statistic, a freak. You stare at the plastic crèche someone has set up on the bar counter and wish your parents hadn't raised you agnostic. It would be nice right now to have recourse to a god of some sort, a god like a traffic cop who shows up and stands in the middle of the road and averts disaster when a stoplight breaks.

You call your mother while you and Molly are making cookies, a tradition your mother started for you when you were eight and Molly, three, could hardly hold a fork. Each year you give your sister a new cookie cutter: swans, bells; once, as a joke, a cross.

"No, I can't handle gizzards," you tell your mother. "We're having salmon."

It was, you realize on this first Christmas without either of them, your parents who defrosted the turkey each year, working their hands over its pale goose-pimpled skin, who thrust their hands up into it to pull out the organs, black and brown and gray. It surprises you now that they never called either of you in and taught you how to dress a turkey. Nor can either of you remember a fight between them, not even bickering. The first time you found your father sleeping in the guest room downstairs you thought he was just sick, or your mother had cramps. You thought this the second time you found him, and the third. You were just out of college then, back living at home, wrapped up in the goose-pimpled skin of your own life. If anyone had asked, you would have described their marriage as happy. Hadn't they renewed their wedding vows just three years earlier, your British grandfather wheezing emphysemically through a passage from "Hiawatha," your Jewish grandfather in tennis whites asking your mother if she'd put on weight?

Over the phone your mother cries a little, you cry a little, you get snot on the sleeve of the new sweater you bought yourself, your only nod to Hanukkah. Molly cookie-cutters two gingerbread girls and squashes them together, reminding you of those insects that copulate and right away die. Your mother makes you promise to fly home for Christmas the following year. It's all too much *loss,* she says, her husband and her marriage and the last of her mother's mind and her home and now her children. She says she wants to read you two a poem from the *New Yorker* about loss, so you get on the extension in your bedroom and listen to your mother read a poem about loss, and it's snowing harder outside and you wonder if right now in your old house in New York your father is standing in the kitchen with his new girlfriend and her two boys, teaching them how to put their hands in the turkey and pull out all in one clean stroke the innards.

Fireflies

Bev's parents are not crazy about flying. For one thing, they say, most pilots these days are drunks. For another, La Guardia is a madhouse, teeming with cops and thieves. This is what they tell her on the way home from the airport.

Bev pulls the car up close to the front of the house. It is a winterized beach house, wedged between summer cottages on Long Island's north shore. Sometimes Bev's daughters call it not a cottage but a shack. In fact, Bev has heard them, in phone conversations with their grandmother, call it exactly that. "It's mosquito season," Bev says. "I say you jump out fast and get indoors."

But her mother does not do anything fast. Clutching a bottle of quinine water in one hand and her big white pocketbook in the other, she climbs out of the car and sniffs the air. "Smells like dead fish out here," she says. She and Bev's father relocated from New York to West Palm Beach a decade ago, and except for the frequent blunt commentary of Manhattanites, they are fully assimilated Floridians, their faces fixed in leathery squints from too much sun.

"The upwind neighbors are clammers," Bev says. Her husband, Emile, has come out to welcome them and help with the luggage.

"They knock down the price because of that smell?" Bev's father paces the length of the car, his hands jammed in the pockets of his tennis shorts.

"Nope," Emile says. "We pay extra for that."

Bev's daughters, M.E. and Caitlin, come outside to greet them. M.E. bolts down the front walk; Caitlin stands on the front steps and gives a limp wave. She is thirteen and bookish, with gold-framed aviator glasses slipping down her nose and a great mass of tangled amber hair. She is just starting to care about what she looks like, and sometimes bursts into tears unprovoked and locks herself in the bathroom. M.E., five years younger, prefers uniform and ceremony, patent leather and charm bracelets. In a white ruffled pinafore and summer sandals, she prances in the driveway, an empty juice bottle in her hands. She has poked holes in the bottle top and plans to catch fireflies.

"Are they out yet?" she asks.

"No, M.E., you cretinous cretin," says Caitlin. "They don't come out till dark."

❖ ❖ ❖

Phyllis rests on the deck out back in a chaise lounge, her bad foot propped up on a seat cushion. Five years ago she slipped in a dinner theater during the intermission of *Guys and Dolls,* and since then she's had both hips replaced. She wears a lift in her right shoe, but this does not correct her unsteady, bobbing gait. Already she has lit a cigarette, which Bev will not tolerate indoors. Bev goes inside and piles bagel chips and lox and whitefish salad on a plate. She hopes her parents won't say anything about her weight. She has been gaining steadily since her thyroid conked out. She imagines she can mark the exact day this happened: last Thanksgiving, between the main course and the pumpkin pie. She lifts a forkful of whitefish salad to her mouth. Out on the deck, her father is interrogating Emile: "What's the tide like out here? Say you have a storm and it rips the whole damn deck off its hinges. Then what?" And she hears Emile's reply: "Well, Bernie, we don't have much in the way of twisters on this part of Long Island."

When she returns, M.E. is scolding Phyllis for smoking. "'Specially Camels," she says. Caitlin blows fake smoke rings from an unlit cigarette. Which shocks Bev more? Caitlin handling the cigarette that deftly or M.E. knowing Camels are a particularly potent brand?

❖ ❖ ❖

Bev got pregnant with Caitlin a month before she married Emile. This was in 1966, when people made coy references to the virgin bride. Bev and Emile still laugh at their inadvertent shotgun wedding. It had been planned down to the smallest detail before Bev ever suspected she might be pregnant, so she never considers herself forced to marry Emile. Phyllis does. Or did. All through Bev's pregnancy, which Bev remembers only as spells of nausea interrupted by spells of vomiting, Phyllis fed Bev noodles and lukewarm tea with the impassivity of a paid attendant. When Emile came home from work, he'd find Bev curled up on the bathroom floor, a string of drool trailing from her open mouth. Phyllis always left just before Emile arrived home. He would see her car retreating as he pulled into the driveway.

No, Phyllis did not approve of Bev's pregnancy. When Bev wore dresses or blouses that showed the curve of her big belly, Phyllis whispered something under her breath that sounded like "shame."

All this changed when Caitlin was born. It was as if the baby had been Phyllis's idea all along. She fed Caitlin formula, then Farina, gave her extravagant gifts (a toy xylophone, a huge floppy rag doll named Lucy Mae); she sided with Caitlin when Caitlin's will conflicted with Bev's. Phyllis and Caitlin invented a game in which Lucy Mae became the culprit for all mischief. "Who let the dog from next door in the house?" Phyllis would say. "Lucy Mae!"

the two of them shouted. "Who filled the washing machine with ping-pong balls?" "Lucy Mae!" Bev, bending to retrieve ping-pong balls from the washing machine, would wonder if her mother might be trying to undermine her.

Of course, Bev now *knows* her mother was trying to undermine her. She can't believe she was ever naive enough to think her mother bought Lucy Mae just for fun.

❖ ❖ ❖

That night, at Bombay Palace, an Indian restaurant where Bev and Emile are longtime regulars, Phyllis orders the early-bird drink special, two martinis for the price of one.

"What are those?" M.E. asks, her hand creeping toward the twin glasses.

"They taste like medicine," Bev says.

"Are they medicine?"

"You could say that," says Phyllis. She sips at her martini. She has a hoarse, rusty laugh that sounds like coughing.

"Don't get too comfortable with that, Phyllis," Bernard says. He is bald and wears a black-and-white baseball cap printed with the name of the country club where he tends grounds. Also, where he chases country club wives. This used to bother Bev, but she's now so appalled at her mother's inactivity, at her refusal even to renew her driver's license, that she thinks of her father's infidelities more as attempts to prove he is still alive. In an aside to Bev, Bernard adds, "She won't drink the second one. She just likes to know it's there. She likes to know there are always martinis to be made for her."

Phyllis drapes a napkin over her pocketbook and keeps it on her lap throughout the meal. "What do you have in there?" M.E. asks. She has recently started carrying one of Bev's old beaded pocketbooks to school.

"All sorts of things," says Phyllis, winking at her.

Bev hopes that doesn't mean candy or nail polish. The sugar

makes the kids crazy, and the smell of nail polish gives her a headache.

"She has a lighter with little shiny gold things on it," M.E. says.

"Would you like it, M.E. honey?" Phyllis pulls back her napkin and snaps open the clasp on her pocketbook, then bends her head to peer into it. Her hair, dyed white-blonde and teased out in tufts, looks to Bev like candle flames, bleached and petrified. There is always this extremity and miscalculation in her mother's appearance, the lipstick too orange, the hair not orange enough.

"Mom," Bev says, "a lighter is no good for an eight year old."

"You're a smarty, aren't you?" Phyllis says to M.E.

"I know the capitals of twenty-two states. Florida: Tallahassee. Most people think it's Miami." M.E. sits up very straight in her chair, a giant round of papadum in her hand.

"No lighter," Bev says. M.E. breaks the papadum in two and, instead of handing half to Bev, takes bites out of both pieces.

As usual, Bev is the one who will end up being the heavy. Emile would only agree to have her parents visit if Bev guaranteed him a position of noninvolvement. He calls it "floating." "For the next forty-eight hours," he said before she left to pick up her parents at the airport, "I'm a floater."

Emile the floater. In his beige shirt and khaki pants, he is unobtrusive as drapes. There was a time when Bev thought he might be color-blind, the way he paired shirts and pants of pale but not identical colors. Now she sees his strategy of blending into the upholstery, whereas she has marked herself out in magenta, a deer in a neon hunter's vest.

Phyllis snaps her pocketbook closed. "You can bet I wouldn't want to be the one to blame if she set herself on fire," she says. "When *Bev* was a little girl, she fell on the patio and cut her head. Bernard still says it's my fault."

Bev wonders how her mother retrieves so many tiny injustices and accidents. In her mother's recounting of them, blame is always neatly laid. Culprits can be traced to bee stings and bleeding foreheads; bland, unsatisfactory meals; even the withering of

Phyllis's favorite dogwood tree in the front yard of the house where Bev grew up. It is the big injustices, the infidelities and separate bedrooms and trips to synagogue alone, that remain vague and incidental, as if no one is to blame.

A waiter comes with the bill. Bev and Emile usually play a game in which each tries to guess the cost of the meal. The one whose guess is closest doesn't have to pay. Bev hopes Emile will just slap down a credit card this evening.

Emile lays his hand across the bill and taps a tooth with one finger. "A hundred and sixty," he says.

Bev makes a grab for the bill. This seems to alert Emile. Even in the dim room, she can see him blush. Emile, the pale engineer in thick glasses who breaks out in hives at weddings and funerals, who blushes at the sound of his own name shouted by one of his daughters in a shopping mall, has realized that since he will be the one paying, his guess must sound more like a brag than a clever estimate.

Luckily, Phyllis and Bernard don't even notice. Ever since they moved into their small Florida condominium, they have reinvented themselves as "poor folks." Phyllis has resuscitated a story about her great-grandmother, the Polish immigrant who pulled her cart of cleaning supplies across the Brooklyn Bridge every morning until her death. Bev does not doubt the truth of this story, but she sees little connection between that woman and her mother, impatiently discarding a mah-jongg tile poolside in West Palm Beach.

❖ ❖ ❖

The old Volvo is a tight squeeze for six people: Emile and Bernard in front, Bev and Phyllis and the two girls in back. Wedged between the car door and Bev, Caitlin presses her face against the window and breathes hard, fogging it up. "I'm suffocating," she moans. She wets her finger and scribbles "Monica + Rick" on the foggy window, then quickly wipes it away. But M.E.

sees what she has written. "Those are just dumb soap opera people," she says. "Why don't you get your own boyfriend?"

"Your brain is so tiny," Caitlin tells her. "You better make sure
it doesn't fall out the next time Dad makes a quick stop."

"She goes to the movies by herself," M.E. says. "She wants us
to think she's with some boy, but I came out of the roller rink on
Saturday and saw her on line all by herself."

"Enough," Bev says. She wants to reach over and slap M.E.,
an urge she hasn't felt since M.E. was much younger and threw
tantrums in department store dressing rooms. In spite of all Bev
and Emile's efforts at raising their children to be cooperative, in-
clusive, democratic, they are still adversaries. When they were
younger, they screamed and pulled each other's hair. Now they
are fighting the way girls learn to fight at school: verbal jabs or
long silences promising treachery, betrayal.

"You watch soaps?" Phyllis asks Caitlin. She leans forward to
see past Bev and M.E. "Which ones?"

Bev has been gauging Caitlin's growing interest in soap op-
eras. Every weekday Caitlin rushes home from school and
comes to a breathless halt in front of the TV. Calling in from
work, Bev hears the impatience in Caitlin's voice: "What is it,
Mom?" Recently, Bev has discovered that Caitlin tape records
episodes. A stack of cassettes, each labeled with the words *General Hospital* and the date of the episode, is burgeoning beneath
Caitlin's bed. Inspecting them, Bev felt sheepish and slightly
nauseated. If I'd had a boy, she thought, would these be pornographic magazines? How do women come to hoard love so
early, and with such secrecy?

"Jesus Christ, Phyllis and those shows," Bernard says. "I
bought her a VCR so she could tape them. It was the only way I
could get her to take the damn dog out for a crap."

Phyllis suddenly joins in. "He bought that dog. I never even
asked for it. The parakeets kept me company just fine."

"Sure," Bernard says. "She covered their cage with a towel

every day at three o'clock so they would think it was night and go to sleep."

"They were tired," Phyllis says.

Caitlin stares out the window again, her finger tracing a heart on the glass that her breath fogs. "M + R," she writes inside the heart. Over and over again she traces, then erases with a single stroke of her hand. Earlier that week, Bev, bringing the laundry down to the basement, discovered Caitlin stretched out on the frayed green sofa. In one hand she held a paperback romance, its bent cover glinting coppery pink. In the other, Emile's electric eraser. A clumsy contraption that always reminded Bev of an overweight dentist's drill, it has gathered dust on Emile's drafting table for years. But there was Caitlin, clutching it in her right hand.

"Whatcha doin'?" Bev asked, faking joviality.

Caitlin blushed, red as Emile in a bind. "Nothing," she said.

Later that day, Bev had gone down again to switch the wash into the dryer and had paused to look at the eraser. It was back on Emile's drafting table, just as he had left it. Bev pressed the "on" button. The machine buzzed fuzzily in her hand. This so surprised her that she almost dropped it. Yet the image that flashed in her mind surprised her more: precocious Caitlin, in her thick-lensed glasses, tentatively touching the top-heavy machine; then, with more assurance, pressing it against her corduroy pants. Bev put the machine down and stared at it. She almost laughed at herself. Her first thought had been, "What would my mother think?"—as if not Caitlin but Bev, who had spent her entire adolescence desperately waiting for a boy to touch her, had committed this forbidden act.

From the outside, Caitlin still looks like the sixth grader who wore white undershirts and chased the ice-cream truck down the block. Her thick pink-tinted glasses make her appear to be goggling at people even when she isn't, and across the roof of her mouth is a palatal expansion device, a silver plate that will widen her jaw, narrowed by seven years of thumb sucking. But she is not a sixth grader anymore. She is wearing a training bra she bought herself. She is reading romance novels on the sly.

Bev wonders now what other kinds of secrets her firstborn will inadvertently reveal. She wants to ask her mother, "Was I like that?" She can't ever remember being so secretive as a girl. In fact, she recalls cataloging entire days to her mother, who chopped chicken or liver in the kitchen while Bev, her red pleated cheerleading skirt swishing across the tops of her thighs as she leapt up for another glass of water, begged to be allowed to go on a date with a basketball player from another high school. Maybe I wore her out with my adolescence, Bev thinks, glancing at her mother trying to doze against the car door. Maybe I told her too much.

❖ ❖ ❖

At home, M.E. wants everyone to go in the hot tub. Emile built it himself into the south end of the deck.

"I'll fall and break my neck," Phyllis says. No one disputes this. Emile gets a lawn chair for Phyllis so she can smoke and watch. M.E. is the first to change into her bathing suit and test the water. At eight, her body is not yet an imposition or an enemy. Caitlin and Bev will take a while longer, trying on several suits and discarding them on their bedroom floors. Caitlin's problem is that right now, she's shaped like a barrel, no curves at all. Bev has tried to reassure Caitlin that this will change, that a woman's body will emerge from all that flesh, like a statue from a marble block. Standing in front of the three-way mirror in her bathroom, though, she's not sure why she went to such lengths to reassure Caitlin, as her own body, nearing middle age, seems to be betraying her, accreting again to blockishness.

When Bev steps out onto the deck, M.E. and Bernard are already in the hot tub. M.E. has dunked her head under, and her hair is freezing in stiff quills. A can of beer sits on the ledge next to Bernard. Emile, in his navy blue bathrobe, is staring at the sky.

"Where's Caitlin?" Bev asks.

"Probably writing up the shows in that notebook." M.E. slicks her hair back from her face. She is sleek as a seal in her red one-piece suit.

Bev stares out into the black water beyond the deck. For some reason she finds the fact that Caitlin keeps a notebook, in addition to the tape recordings, foreboding. "What does she write in her notebook?" she asks, knowing that if M.E. knows, she will tell.

M.E. shrugs. "She probably just talks about the different ladies on the show and what they're wearing."

Bev smiles. This, she realizes, is the kind of notebook M.E. would keep, if she were ever inclined to do such a thing. She suspects Caitlin's notebook contains nothing of the kind.

"C'mon in, Bev," Bernard says. "Water won't get any wetter."

Bev hesitates. She wants Caitlin to be an ally, to be imperfect along with her. Her sixty-seven-year-old father is still tanned and tightened from playing tennis and prowling after young Florida wives. "I'll go see about Caitlin," Bev says.

She pauses outside Caitlin's door and listens. "Ready?" she asks.

"Inaminute." This comes sullenly through the door.

Bev decides she will wait, even if Caitlin is simply sitting on her bed, hoping Bev will go away. Finally the door swings open and out slumps Caitlin in a denim jacket and cutoffs. She casts Bev a dark look and says, "I only wear bathing suits for *swimming*." She heads straight out to the deck. Bev watches her retreat.

The door to Caitlin's room still stands ajar. On impulse, Bev goes in. The blond wood bookshelf Emile built several years ago is crammed with books. No kitschy smiling dolls or porcelain puppies for Caitlin. Before Bev knows exactly what she's doing, she's scanning the bookshelf, stooping to peer under the bed, wedging her hand between the mattress and the box spring. Here she finds it—a battered blue spiral notebook. In Caitlin's close, careful handwriting, Bev reads: "March 20—

They depositioned Monica and she had to tell the truth about her affair with Rick." Following that, in thick capital letters: "MY PREDICTION IS ALAN WILL GET HIS HANDS ON THE DEPOSITION AND STRANGLE HER. IF MONICA DIES I MIGHT HAVE TO KILL MYSELF." The notebook is filled with passages of dialogue between Monica and Rick, meticulously reproduced, torrid and anguished.

Bev stuffs the notebook back where she found it and pauses to take a deep breath. She imagines Caitlin, sturdy and competent, slipping a noose around her neck, kicking a chair out from under her. Caitlin methodically emptying a bottle of Valium, as if following doctor's orders to take all fifty pills at once. Bev is troubled by the clarity and ease with which these images come to her. Why is Caitlin obsessed with a love affair between two starchy doctor characters in their forties? Why not some long-haired punk with an electric guitar and dimples?

She is relieved to find Caitlin dangling her feet in the hot tub. Yet as Bev climbs in, she looks at the water and thinks, Drowning. Caitlin's tangled hair and knobby white knees look tragic and possibly dangerous. When Caitlin was a baby, everything seemed so burdened with the potential of disaster that Bev sometimes blockaded herself and Caitlin in the living room and stayed indoors all day. She has not looked at the world this way for years—M.E. never needed or wanted such close supervision—but now everything seems capable of helping Caitlin harm herself.

"You still taking those thyroid pills?" Bernard asks, scrutinizing Bev in her ice-blue bathing suit.

"They were giving me heart palpitations."

"So? What's a little palpitating?" Bernard says. "Isn't that why we all like falling in love?"

Bev pictures her father rolling around on a motel bed with a fake redhead, lipstick smeared on her front teeth. She wonders whether the women mind that he's bald. "I felt like I had a speedboat racing through my aorta," she says.

"Hey, rocket scientist," Bernard calls to Emile, who has fixed four gin and tonics in paper cups. "If you geniuses can invent a hot tub that cleans itself, how about some pills for your wife's weight?"

Bev thinks she might burst into tears. She knows Emile won't rescue her tonight: he's floating. M.E.'s head is underwater again; she's counting how many seconds she can stay down before coming up for air. And Caitlin, trailing one listless hand in the water, might be plotting her suicide just this minute. Bev wonders how she ever could have imagined Caitlin would be her ally.

"He's drinking too much," Phyllis says. She snuffs out her cigarette on the sole of her shoe and tosses it over the deck railing. "Stop drinking so much, Bernard."

"Okay, all right," Bernard says, holding his hands in the air.

Caitlin says something under her breath which Bev is sure only she hears. From Caitlin's mouth, the word sounds like an incantation: "philanderer." Philanderer? Probably Caitlin learned it from her soap opera. It is not a word kids use. It's not even a word that adults use in real life. For real infidelity it's too dramatic, too precise.

"I am now going to give my tap dancing recital," M.E. announces, scrambling out of the hot tub. She wraps a towel around her narrow waist and dashes indoors. She returns in tap shoes and white ruffled ankle socks, a white headband in her wet hair. Tossing her towel over the back of a chair, she clasps her hands behind her back, and in her bright bathing suit, begins to dance.

Bev watches her younger daughter's thin, fast, white legs, her feet slapping like castanets against the redwood floorboards of the deck. At one time, she thinks, I was that agile.

"Join in when you know the words," M.E. calls sweetly, playing her audience. She has begun singing "Tea for Two." Bernard is the only one who joins in. He climbs out of the hot tub and improvises a little barefoot soft-shoe beside her, his towel draped around his neck. When they finish their dance, M.E. curtsies and Bernard swings her up on his hip, always the man to court the prettiest, slimmest girl. In the only photo Bev can recall of her parents as a young couple, sepia-toned and labeled "Coney Island, 1938," her father, bare to the waist, easily holds her tiny mother, demure and pleased in a gingham-skirted bathing suit.

"You're my movie star dancer," Bernard tells M.E. "You're Ginger Rogers."

In Bernard's arms, M.E. offers an indulgent smile to some imagined crowd, though she clearly has no idea who Ginger Rogers is. Phyllis allows herself a single comment on the performance: "You're a couple of show-offs." To Bev she says, "You've got yourself another performer." She taps her cigarette on the metal elbow rest of her chair.

No, Bernard wants nothing to do with her mother's limp, her clunky orthopedic shoes, her patient sideways plodding down staircases. Bev thinks she will always picture her mother as she is now, stranded in a lawn chair, smoking with the studied indifference of someone who has never been the star of the show. Caitlin and Emile sit quietly outside the immediate circle cast by the single outside light, Emile nursing his gin and tonic, Caitlin intent on picking the lint off a towel. Moths hum in a flurry around the light.

M.E. and Bernard are practicing their next dance, within hearing distance but not paying attention. Bev wishes she could cook up some unimportant but absorbing distraction; even the mittens that resisted her attempts to teach herself to knit this past winter would be welcome right now.

"For God's sake," Phyllis says. "You wonder how we all got stuck with each other." She tilts her head toward the hot tub. "The two of them aping around like they're in a circus." She leans toward Bev and cups her hand around her mouth. "Be glad you have Caitlin."

❖ ❖ ❖

Caitlin and M.E. have gotten into their nightgowns. Bev stands in the hallway and listens to Bernard and M.E. play Chutes and Ladders in M.E.'s bedroom. M.E. shrieks every time she rolls the dice. In Caitlin's room, Phyllis and Caitlin are leafing through a copy of *Soap Opera Digest*. Bev tries to recall when it was that Caitlin lost interest in the "Stories for Free Children" Bev always clipped out of *Ms.* magazine and started spending her allowance on *Soap Opera Digest*.

"See him?" Phyllis is saying to Caitlin. "He's the biggest two-timer around. He was two-timing with one of his nurses in 1968, when I first started watching."

"Yeah, and they still give him the best-looking girlfriends," Caitlin says. "No way would those girls go out with an old guy like him in real life."

Bev halts at this, pleased. Caitlin must not believe that her soap opera heroine will actually be asphyxiated.

"Oh, Cait," Phyllis says. "Men like that always get young girls." There is the sound of her lighter flint striking and catching, then the whish of exhaled breath. She is smoking in the house.

"Can I try that?" Caitlin whispers, so low that Bev can barely hear.

"Don't tell your mother."

"I won't."

Bev stands perfectly still and listens. There is a deep breath in, then a fit of coughing and the thump of Phyllis's hand on Caitlin's back. "You took too much," Phyllis is saying. "You can't breathe in so deep."

Bev, still in her wet bathrobe, wants to barge into Caitlin's bedroom, snuff out the cigarette, get Caitlin to promise she won't kill herself. But she feels inert, filled with water. Her mother and Caitlin have been allies ever since the day Caitlin learned to crawl.

"Can I try your lighter?" Caitlin is asking. "The one M.E. likes."

The clasp on Phyllis's purse snaps open again, and Bev

knows, without hearing it, that her mother is placing the lighter in Caitlin's open hand, and that Caitlin won't have to give it back.

"This is cool," Caitlin says. "Thanks."

They are kissing each other good night. Bev stands rooted in the dim hallway, knowing she will have to go looking for the lighter tomorrow, knowing that tonight she will dream of Caitlin's amber hair flickering orange and blue in a burst of flames as she disappears into the dark; her empty blue room, the spiral notebook, the narrow bed: all luminous, about to ignite.

Lily's the Maid

1

After Gretchen was born, Susanna felt life become very large. Life became as large and out of proportion as her body had felt those nine months when Gretchen was growing inside her. So much was demanded of a mother. So much was demanded of a wife, and Susanna had to be that, too, though all her plans from youth had organized themselves around the notion that she would be a public figure, someone who had opinions and got asked, frequently, to voice them.

Even when she and Carl and Gretchen packed up and moved away from Washington, D.C., with its protests and monuments, to a small seaside town on the north shore of Long Island, the feeling of having a life foisted on her that so little resembled any of the extraordinary lives she had imagined for herself (she had pictured travel; she had pictured lecture podiums) persisted.

She had not expected any of it—marriage, motherhood, small-town life—to be so exhausting.

This was in the late sixties, when they left D.C. And then it was the seventies, Long Island, quieter times. Maybe it was not so quiet other places.

She had never lived in a small town before. On parade

holidays, everyone turned out on the town's main road with aluminum chairs they set up along the sidewalk. After a number of years, Susanna began to suspect that the parade crowd that turned out was exactly the same every year. The same fossilized Veterans of Foreign Wars limping by in the same aging white convertible, the same mayor wearing a scarlet sash diagonally across his chest with MAYOR printed on it. The same band with silver xylophones propped up by invisible devices at their waists. The Comanche Raiders, that was the name of the band despite the fact that only two or three of perhaps forty men had the burnished skin and dark eyes of real Indians. The rest were white men with wire-framed glasses and stubborn chins. But all of them wore headdresses and bright beaded jackets, and on their feet were the soft-soled moccasins that Susanna promised to find and buy for herself, though each year brought her only the unfulfilled reminder from the previous year. Gretchen always, when the Comanche Raiders approached, grabbed at Susanna's hand and tugged it with pushy, childish terror.

But it could not have been the same parade crowd every year: Susanna had to remember to scold herself so that she would not walk around believing such things. She could not go around believing that time did not inch forward in its reliable, inexorable way. Wasn't it true each year that Gretchen grew larger? The feet for which Susanna bought patent leather shoes at the beginning of each year could not even be coaxed into their casings at year's end. And Gretchen was no longer throwing tantrums like a wild little animal. She answered questions in complete sentences and demonstrated aptitude with numbers and concepts, like an actual person. And weren't the basement and the attic a little more cluttered each year, a little more resistant to the boxes full of Gretchen's old clothes that Susanna carried up or down, for she could never remember whether she was supposed to be keeping Gretchen's old clothes in the basement or the attic. And, finally, wasn't it true that the feverish cluster of feelings that had led her, Susanna, to Carl in the first place—didn't that cluster diminish within her a little bit with each passing year, so that after five, or seven, or however many years it had been, the cluster at first so ripe and full it might have been a real cluster of grapes, boiled itself down to a few granules of sugar?

But all of these things came to be so gradually, and over what felt like such a long period of time, that Susanna had difficulty believing they were true unless she happened on a photo of herself with Carl. Then she would see her arms thrown around Carl's neck, the rapt expression on her face when she looked at him—he made her blush, she could see, even in the black-and-white photos she could see it—and she would remember precisely how her whole body had felt full of fire when she and Carl were first together, as if all the ways into her body—the mouth, the ears, the nose, the shy rectum, the sighing vagina—were about to ignite. That was the way of her desire. And then, at some point, it was not.

❖❖❖

There was a time in Susanna's life when she smoked marijuana and came to feel ill and not smart enough to discuss communism and capitalism in the way that other people in the room were able to criticize the clothes they were wearing and the bottles of beer waiting for them in the refrigerator.

There was a time when she and her friend Donya took a Trailways bus to a march in support of abortion rights and some counterprotesters threw a cloth doll soaked in something that looked like real blood in the direction of a woman wheeling twins in a stroller, so that she and Donya, marching just behind the woman, ran forward and grabbed the doll and hurled it back at them. She, Susanna, was angry then.

There was a time when she attended a country day school, where the girls were required to wear pinafores with white aprons over them, the boys starched shirts and lederhosen. That made her angry, too, those charades.

There was a time when she stood on the sidewalk and watched the Comanche Raiders march past with their xylophones gleaming in the sun, and there was a time when she and Carl went to Parents' Night at Gretchen's school and sat crammed and close to the floor beside other parents at the desks where their children sat all day, bored or lonesome or thirsty.

A time came when Susanna could no longer bring herself to climb out of bed and perform the daily ablutions: the washing of the body, the brushing of the teeth, the changing of the bra and underwear (there was a stretch during this time when she slept in her bra and underwear, Carl not saying anything and not trying to unhook the bra or push his fingers beneath the elastic waistband of the underwear). Then all these times were past, and she could not arrange them in the order in which they had occurred, though it seemed important to be able to do so.

Carl, standing amid the tangle of nightgowns and socks she had let fall beside their bed, surveyed her one evening. He said, "You could hire a maid."

She had a bachelor's degree in sociology that she had never used: Gretchen had come along before she got the chance. She began to volunteer at a shelter for abused women. Terrible things had been done to them. But the laws were not good; there was not much anyone could do for the women except try to keep them away from the men who beat them. And it was true that in spite of whatever threats and maulings had been visited upon them, the women almost always wanted to get back together with their husbands or boyfriends. Once things blew over, they would get back together. All of them believed things would blow over. It did not matter that the part of the upper arm where you would tap or grasp someone you recognized in a crowd had been burned with an iron or slashed with a knife. Or that lit cigarettes had been pressed into the soft flesh of the hand between the thumb and forefinger. Everyday objects, objects one admired for the ingenuity of their human inventors and the ease of use they provided, had been turned on the women. The handles of umbrellas. Golf clubs. Corkscrews. Spoons. Jesus, corkscrews. You wanted to laugh when you heard the stories the women told. Sometimes they were laughing when they finally managed to explain what had been done to them.

With the golf club.

And then there would be a little pause.

Then after. I suppose he hit me with it after.

Sometimes they would not be so sure of what had happened to them. Then there would be the high, hysterical laughter of someone putting things behind her. Hair had been torn right out of their heads; fists socked into stomachs led to miscarriages that put an end to babies conceived in spite of resistance. Oh, but everything would turn out all right. The optimism of the women cowed Susanna, the optimism and goodwill and foolishness.

The shelter had a storefront that advertised itself as an insurance company. The entrance opened onto a corridor with a locked door at the end and a glass panel that allowed the receptionist to view visitors. All men who were unfamiliar had to be screened. As for the women clients who came for counseling or shelter, they were not allowed to have male visitors at all, even if the woman claimed to have called the man and begged him to visit.

Susanna hired one of the women. Not to work at the shelter; she didn't have the power to hire people there. She hired her as her maid. The woman had no money and no formal education beyond some high school, but Susanna felt she was not a lost cause. She had no children yet, it seemed, and she wavered back and forth about whether she felt her boyfriend had really abused her. Some of the ones at the shelter weren't even able to do that.

Her name was Lily.

She carried a white purse with a gold clasp on it. Whenever they got into talking about Arturo, Lily snapped the clasp of the purse open and took out a compact. Then she would pat powder on her face.

"You let him do things you didn't want to do," Susanna said.

Lily looked at Susanna, a little incredulous. "Where do *you* live?"

For years Susanna would think about that sentence. When she looked back, it seemed that, for all the events of her life that had and would come, she marked out a time line according to the moment she hired Lily. Before Lily. After Lily.

Lily Estivera. Lily. A flower. She was from Costa Rica—Susanna wasn't even sure she could locate Costa Rica on a map—and her English was as good as her Spanish. She could not have been more than twenty years old when Susanna hired her.

She told Susanna about the hairline fracture to the skull, the broken fingers, the eye that had swelled up like a plum. Better those than memories of herself whimpering, submitting.

2

"You don't have to bother with Gretchen's room. Or our bedroom. I did them yesterday," Susanna told her. They were standing in Susanna's kitchen, which was as clean as the rooms she mentioned.

"Why do you do them yesterday if you know I am coming today?" Lily said. She was affecting a way of talking that Susanna recognized: English as spoken by a person from a Spanish-speaking country, though Lily had never spoken English with an accent.

"I didn't want you to think I was a slob," Susanna said.

"I think you're a slob if you do the work and then pay me for it."

"Okay. You'll eat a piece of toast. Some marmalade. Coffee."

Lily sat down on the stool Susanna indicated and accepted the toast and coffee. She had her hair pulled up in an elaborate barrette that did not look capable of holding the hair in place. And yet it was. A coil of hair looped up and sprayed out above the barrette like a cascade of black satin. It was her underbite that Susanna found interesting; it made her look both insolent and flawed, the way objects made by hand are more endearing if they have visible imperfections. The underbite, and she was short-waisted, though in an appealing and compact way, with a full shelf of bosom. It looked swollen. *Bosom.* Susanna had never thought to describe anyone to herself as having a bosom. Hadn't *bosom* gone the way of *vixen* and *wench*? And yet, looking at Lily, she couldn't help but think of the word. Perhaps Lily did after all have a child already, a nursing baby. Perhaps Lily hadn't wanted to tell her; the situation with Arturo was already bad enough.

Then another thought came to Susanna. *Oh how I would like to be that baby.* The thought popped into her head, just like that.

Once you have such a thought, the best you can do is let it float. You can try to retract it, stomp it into an unrecognizable pulp, bash it shut, pretend it didn't come flittering out of you, but you cannot forget or deny that you had it.

Here she was, a woman with a maid. Here she was, a woman feeling interested in the bosom of a woman who was going to clean her toilets and shake out her rugs. First she had become a woman, and that had been hard for her to believe. Then a woman with a husband. A woman with a baby. A mother. Packing the canned puddings and sandwiches with the crusts cut off into a lunch box for Gretchen to take to school, hadn't she longed to pinch herself awake from the strange dream of motherhood, cluttered with Gretchen's tantrums and white containers of baby powder, their shaker tops somehow clogged with a dense invisible substance that did not allow the powder easily to sift through? You had to jimmy it and coax it, and then, when you were no longer expecting it, a cloud of powder would issue from the container like a sneeze.

But now Lily. Now no more tantrums from Gretchen, no baby powder with its cloying smell of false flowers. Now when Gretchen got a fever or a bellyache or the unbearable itching in the corners of the eyes, or any of the finicky little ailments to which neither Susanna nor the pediatrician could assign a name, Gretchen could fetch her own sticky bottle of cough syrup, her own ointment and tissues. Gretchen at school, Carl at work all the time, Susanna with a maid.

"It doesn't look to me like you need any help," Lily said, glancing around. "What would I do?"

"Oh, you'll find things," Susanna said, in an airy, quavering voice she did not intend.

She excused herself and went into the bathroom. In the mirror she assessed the person into whom she had made herself. This person wore a navy blue sweater dress with a false collar made of lace. It was the fashion then to attach false collars to shirts and dresses, to fancy them up. The navy blue dress had shoulder pads that gave Susanna the look of someone—a woman—trying to give off an impression of power. The effect she was trying for was stern and unyielding, which were the traits she associated with power. But the false collar undermined all that. She took it off. Her hair was very carefully attended to, dyed a reddish brown that did not especially suit her and did not look like any color her hair had ever been. What color had her hair been when it was her natural hair color? Her eyebrows did not give her a hint, as they were also reddish brown, dyed at the suggestion of the woman who cut Susanna's hair. She was very pretty and stylish, the sort of woman who can dispense advice to other women, any sort of advice at all, and not be challenged, so compelling is the example she presents. All manner of dyeing and waxing and tweezing gets accomplished by such women. But the dyeing of the eyebrows had not been a good idea; it made this person looking back from the mirror seem wolfish and expectant. Her hair was as stiff and purposeful as the shoulder pads; it had no natural inclination anymore to fall around her face. Instead, the strands were held off her face by a metal clip shaped like a butterfly.

She reached back and released the spring mechanism on the clip. The clip was in her hand—a dragonfly, actually. She shook her head. First gently, then vigorously, as if she were a child refusing to budge from her spot. The two wings of hair she had pulled back off her face sagged slightly but retained their overall shape, two wings of hair swooping up and back, as if waiting obediently for the dragonfly to soar up and secure them to her head again.

There was so much waste in the world, this dress and this hair and these eyebrows and this dragonfly clip. She should stop dyeing her hair and her eyebrows and let them return to their natural color; she should stop wearing shoulder pads.

She was at this time twenty-eight.

The dragonfly clip floated in the toilet water for a tentative, triumphant moment, then sank to the bottom of the bowl.

3

Gretchen was standing in the middle of her bedroom and working on something in her nose. You were not supposed to pick your nose in public, but in private, if you had something caught and bothering you, you could get it out and wipe it in a tissue.

"Digging for gold?"

Lily was leaning in the doorway. She had the spray polish and rags in her hands.

"No." Gretchen whipped her hand down to her side and curled the finger into her palm. It was possible that her nose was going to bleed. The tissues were on the dresser, on the other side of the room.

"Hasn't your mother ever told you not to do that?"

"I wasn't doing anything."

"I caught you."

Was that where the dislike of Lily began?

"I'll tell your mama." Lily pushed off from the doorway with her hip and swung the rag artfully, flipping her wrist.

"Tell her whatever you want."

Lily squinted at her, the way she squinted at the countertops to see if they were spotless. "It's bleeding now. You've made it bleed."

After that, Gretchen made messes wherever she liked. She had a game with little multicolored pegs that plugged into a black screen. A light bulb behind the screen illuminated the pegs, so that you could make a pattern with the pegs and then light it up. After Lily made the remark about gold digging, Gretchen didn't mind so much if she left the pegs scattered all over the floor. Or she would eat tuna on toast and leave the crusts and the plate and maybe a glass with an inch of milk in it on the dresser. For days she would leave it, since, at first, Lily came only on Fridays.

The pegs got returned to the box they came in, the plates and glasses removed to the kitchen.

Then one day her mother said, "You need to do some cleaning up before Lily gets here."

"Lily's the maid."

"Lily is the housekeeper," her mother said, "and it is not her responsibility to pick up your moldy leftovers."

And some time after that, Lily came for dinner. These were nights when Gretchen's father was away in Delaware or D.C. on a business trip. Her mother would be up from the table to get the hot sauce for Lily and then up from the table again to get a glass of water for Lily and then up to open another bottle of wine if she and Lily finished the one she opened when Lily arrived.

Then at the third dinner Lily broke a glass.

"Go get the broom and the dustpan," her mother said. "Get Lily another glass."

Gretchen stared at her mother.

"You heard what I said."

"She did it. Why do I have to fix it?"

"Because you're ten and Lily's tired."

"I'll get it, señorita," Lily said. She was already on her feet; she knew where to find the broom and the dustpan and another glass.

"Go to your room," her mother said.

"It doesn't matter, Susanna. I did it," Lily said.

"I said go to your room."

Gretchen stood up and pushed her chair back noisily from the table. There was a small piece of turkey on her plate that she was saving for last. She went to lift it into her mouth.

"Hey." Her mother slapped her hand back down on her plate. Her hand got gravy on the palm, which she wiped down her shirt as she walked to her room.

Susanna.

Señorita.

That was the beginning.

❖❖❖

At the Memorial Day parade, her mother and Lily stood behind her, talking. Already Gretchen could feel in the pavement beneath her feet a gathering tremor; the parade would round the bend in the road any moment. But neither her mother nor Lily was watching for her father, who would be marching with the Elks Club, and Gretchen was not yet tall enough to see who was coming down the road until they marched right past her. She was afraid she was going to miss him.

"Maybe I'll meet somebody nice," Lily said.

The honking horns of the parade came and drowned out all the other sounds for a good long moment.

"You watch out for nice," her mother said.

"I'm a big girl," said Lily.

Gretchen saw her father march past with the other men in the Elks Club. He waved in her direction, but he also waved in all the other directions, and he didn't mouth her name that she could see. Her father would always, her whole life, be this remote waving figure, his affections so diffuse that she would feel by the time she was an adolescent that any daughter could have been assigned to him, anyone would have been fine.

After the parade, her mother and Lily drove her to meet her father at the beach. All the beaches in the village were pebble beaches and required tough skin on the soles of the feet. Gretchen was able to dash nimbly to the water's edge. When she looked back, her mother was leaning on Lily's arm as she made her way down toward the water. She had her sandals dangling from the fingers of one hand, as it was no use trying to wear sandals on a pebble beach. All the rocks and pebbles and broken shells just cascaded in under your heels. So her mother was stepping with her bare feet on the pebbles, as if stepping through fire. She was complaining, though Gretchen was far enough away from them that she could only see the contortions of her mother's mouth, not hear the sounds that went along with them.

Hold on, señorita, hold on. Those were the words coming out of Lily's mouth.

It was hot for late May, with people throwing Frisbees to each other in the water and some teenage girls lying on their bellies with their bikini tops unhooked.

"Easy to learn," her father said. He was watching two boys climb onto a small sailboat. He explained something about centerboards and capsizing. Gretchen couldn't pay enough attention to understand what he was talking about. She was watching her mother and Lily, who reached the water's edge and greeted them, Lily dancing happily on a patch of wet sand.

"My feet, my aching feet," Lily said. Then she danced in a circle and sang

*There's a place in France
where the girls wear paper pants
and the pants they wear
are guaranteed to tear*

She sang it with the Spanish accent.

"She'll get us all thrown out," Gretchen's father said. He was lying on his back on a towel and looking up at Lily, but not with ardor. He might have been trying to figure out how to launch her off into some other family's company.

"Stop ogling her," her mother said.

Her father shut his eyes. "Believe you me, sister," he said.

Her mother shook a blanket down on the pebbles and opened her straw bag. In it were tangerines, Lily's cigarettes, her lighter, baby oil. This was when people still covered themselves with baby oil, before sunblock. There were other sunbathers holding silver reflector boards in their laps. Her mother took out the baby oil and handed Lily the cigarettes and the lighter. When they were finished, Gretchen reached in for a tangerine. The skin of the fruit was warm, and inside, the fruit felt almost hot when she put it in her mouth. She fed herself each crescent with the mechanical precision of someone being ordered to eat as she watched her mother and Lily take off the clothes they had worn to the parade. Underneath, her mother was wearing a red bikini with a white ring of plastic in the center of the chest that seemed to hold the whole arrangement together. Lily's was a string bikini, black and white, zebra-striped. Each of them was rubbing baby oil on her own belly, her mother in the ashamed, self-conscious way Gretchen would later recognize as the way of most adult women. Lily, too, was rubbing oil carefully on her stomach, but not in deference to shame or ugliness or fat.

Marks. A discolored area on her stomach like a faded painting of a pomegranate.

"I got hit," Lily said.

No one said anything for a few seconds. Gretchen's father, lying with his arm over his eyes, sat up and blinked against the sunlight. "What's this?" he asked.

"Her stomach," her mother said.

Lily arched her back so that the faded pomegranate stretched out into full view.

"That's certainly a thing," her father said, looking away. He might have been looking away as much from her mother's earlier ogling comment as he was from distaste or good manners.

"You should have seen what the other guy looked like," Lily said.

Then both of Gretchen's parents asked questions at the same time.

"Is she one of those from the shelter?" her father asked.

"Are you crazy?" her mother said.

"Yes," said Lily, "and no."

Gretchen pictured the walloping you would have to get to end up with a pomegranate like that. Lily, getting a good wallop. It made her almost glad.

4

Someone was playing "Turkey in the Straw." It was coming on evening; it felt all day as if it had been coming on evening. Carl said that was just how it felt when you got high.

This was 1968.

"Is it supposed to feel like all your heads are coming out of black velvet?" Susanna asked, and everybody laughed. She was the only one in the room who had never gotten high. She meant that their heads looked to her as if they were mounted on black velvet: comic, majestic busts.

"It's like it's three-dimensional," she said. She was not sure if she said it out loud.

"It *is* three-dimensional," one of the bearded guys said.

Then she went into another phase of it. The black velvet went away and got replaced. She felt as if she could see every person in the room exactly as he or she really was. She could see all their essences.

Donya was sitting at the end of the sofa. She was the one playing "Turkey in the Straw." She could see in Donya's essence that she was all clear and that she loved her, Susanna, in a way that if you used language to convey it would be something like wholeheartedly.

Carl was another story.

"You are another story," she told Carl.

She was about to tell Carl what he was. She saw a dark light going through the center of him, something opaque and leaden. She was trying to figure out how to put some words to this.

Carl was sitting in the rocking chair. This was her parents' house. They were away for a weekend, in Hilton Head. She had invited all these people to come hang out in her parents' house. She was twenty-two.

Donya leaned over. The ends of her hair brushed Susanna's forehead. "Don't," she whispered.

A little while later she felt good enough to sit up and ask for a glass of water. Carl went and came back with a beer.

"I asked for a glass of water."

"This will do you better."

Carl was one of the smart ones from high school who went on to Cornell. He had just graduated and was letting his hair grow. Men were doing this all of a sudden. In her bedroom, she told him she liked how he was growing his hair. At the holidays, when they saw each other, he had always had it clipped very short. He sat down at her desk chair and held her on his lap, and she told him about what it had been like at the University of Southern Florida, with the unrest and the separate drinking fountains. Also how the women at the university had ten o'clock curfews on weekends but the men were allowed to stay out until twelve.

"That's probably for your protection," he said gravely.

She said she didn't think it was fair. As she was saying it, he kissed her.

"I always wanted to go on a date with you in high school," he said. His voice was trembling. "I never told you that."

Her heart sped up when someone flattered her.

"I'm glad we're done with college," he said.

She tried not to shift too much on his lap. She didn't want him to think she was trying to provoke him.

"I didn't think you'd go," he said. It took her a moment to figure out he was back to talking about high school.

"I would've," she said. It didn't sound as convincing as she'd intended.

"Do you think we could sit on that bed? I'd like to lean on the wall," he said.

She jumped up and let him take her hand as they walked to

the bed. Some time passed before what he said to her struck her as odd. And later, when she thought about it, she thought he must have been drunk, to want to lean on the wall.

A time came when they were lying beside each other with their heads on her pillow.

"I want you so much, Susanna," he said. He took her hand and pressed it against his erection.

She would have a good laugh about that later, with Donya. *I want you so much.* What a badly scripted line. And the erection, offered up to her as some kind of proof. "*Sheep* give men erections," Donya said. "And motorcycles! Motorcycles do."

She only told Donya part of it.

Other parts she saved.

It seemed for a while that Carl fell asleep. His breathing got slow and regular, his chest rising and falling under her hand. She began to wonder, lying there, if he still had the erection.

She would touch it, just to see.

She misjudged the distance. It was right there, straining at the rough weave of his underwear.

"Oh," he said. "Oh, god."

"What?"

He pushed himself up on his elbow. "Just that it's terrible," he said. "All the things I want to do are terrible."

"Like what?"

He seemed to be considering how to phrase what he was going to say next.

"I want you to take it in your mouth," he said.

She didn't say anything.

"That's dirty, isn't it? That's what you're thinking."

"Yes," she said. But she hadn't been thinking it was dirty. Rather, that she wanted to know how it would feel. Also if she would be able to get out of it if she tried it and didn't like it. If she gagged. That was something she didn't know how to ask.

"Okay, we won't," he said, and lay back.

But the lying back like that still seemed to suggest an invitation. She tucked her hair behind her ears.

"I think I might be able to," she said.

"Don't say anything."

She worked at his underwear, which was awkward.

"Ooh," he gasped, when her mouth was over it. She just leaned down and put her mouth around the whole length of his penis; she had no idea of teasing or style.

He pushed it toward the back of her throat and then away from her, so that it would have popped out of her mouth if she didn't follow it.

"Ooh, god," he said. His voice seemed to be coming from somewhere above her. "I don't think I can do this without fucking you."

No one had ever said "fucking" to her like that. She was surprised to hear it out of his mouth, a Cornell graduate. She felt a marvelous, frightening sense of arousal. She had absolutely no words to communicate any of this to him.

"Do you want to?" he asked.

After he got on top of her, everything changed. She didn't want to do more things to him, and she didn't want him to do any more things to her. She wanted them to go back to the early part, with just the kissing. Later, she would wonder if that was the way with all women the first time, or if it was the pot she had smoked, or something about him.

"Carl?" she said.

"What?" He sounded, suddenly, gruff. Or distracted, as if he had something going on that didn't include her.

"Carl?"

"Jesus, what?"

"I don't think I can do this."

"We're already doing it," he said.

He hadn't stopped moving inside her during all this.

"Carl, stop. I said I don't want to."

"Oh, *god*," Carl said. He collapsed on his elbows, his head

bumping into one of her shoulders. She thought that he was col-
lapsing because he was annoyed with her, or because he was hurt.
She didn't have any idea what a man's orgasm might look like.

She didn't understand what had happened until she got the
news from the doctor, about the baby.

5

By the time Gretchen got to high school, there was a regular unit
on sex education, less coy and more useful than in her parents'
day. It was treated as a practical matter alongside other practical
matters: alcoholism, drug abuse, first aid.

Now, though, most of what she remembers from back then
had to do with treating a snakebite. Also how to tie a tourniquet.
And if you took PCP, there was a good chance you would jump
through a plate glass window or drown in an inch of your own
vomit. It wasn't until a few years later that a unit got added about
AIDS. That wasn't a concern yet, back when Gretchen was in
high school.

A day came, then, when her mother insisted on sitting her
down for a talk. "Boys will want to do things," she began. She
was actually sitting down on Gretchen's bed, patting the space
beside her.

"I know, I know," Gretchen said. She remembers how eager
she was to fend off explanations. "They talked about it at school."

"Well, isn't that good news?" her mother said. She tilted her
head to one side, waiting, it seemed, for Gretchen to give an
account of what she had learned. That's how she had been since
the end of Lily, attentive and chipper and blank.

Lily had come to dinner all the time after the Memorial Day
parade that year. Then toward the end of one winter there was a
warm day in February when everyone went out in short-sleeved
shirts. It was clear Lily wasn't just putting on weight.

And then one day, a couple of months later than that,

Gretchen's mother came home from work in the middle of the afternoon and undressed and got into bed.

"Turn that off," she said to Gretchen, who was sitting on the floor watching *General Hospital*. Gretchen was just in from school herself; she hadn't even taken her coat off yet.

"Are you sick or something?" she asked her mother.

"I said turn that filth off."

Gretchen remembers how reluctantly she obeyed. How she dawdled and fumed. The story line that had her interest involved a young woman who got raped in a disco by an older man. After that she ran off and had a torrid affair with him. The man was not at all attractive: it looked as if he had some sort of artificial hair transplant. Hair plugs, they were called. They looked to Gretchen like the connections she imagined they put on you if you were going to be fried in the electric chair. The girl, Laura, was very pretty in a way that to Gretchen somehow compensated for, or at least complicated, the man's ugliness. A pretty woman with an ugly man always did.

"He killed her," her mother said flatly, when Gretchen was done turning off the TV.

For a minute, Gretchen didn't know who her mother was talking about.

"Lily." On her side in bed, her mother pulled up her knees. Gretchen sat down on the floor again and leaned against the bed. It had begun to shake. She watched the TV screen, all dark. She stared at it anyway, for a long time, almost believing that the force of her attention would return her to the scene she was missing. She was only fourteen then, too paralyzed by adolescence to get up and do anything for her mother. A teenager, then. She tries, now, these years later, to remember that.

I'm from Ballymullet

TIDY TOWN PARALYZED BY PROMISCUOUS TOURIST

Three-time first-prize winner in Ireland's Tidy Towns competition, the drowsy seaside town of Ballymullet may never again be a tourist's paradise. In the midst of this idyllic landscape of thatched roofs and quaint pubs set against a backdrop of green hills dotted with sheep, a silent killer lurks. Or so says Father Brendan Lenehan, the priest who shocked parishioners at the Mary of Magdalene Church in Ballymullet last Sunday, when he announced that a female tourist from England had infected several local men with HIV, the virus that causes AIDS.

The residents of Ballymullet, long accustomed to the presence of tourists in their pubs and shops, have until now welcomed outsiders. Yet in an interview this week, Father Lenehan speculated that the moral backwardness tourists bring with them is threatening the way of life enjoyed by locals in this remote hamlet. "The end of our innocence is being ushered in with an event of near biblical proportions," Father Lenehan declared. "Sex and drugs can only lead us down the road to plague and pestilence."

Jimmy Faye

Afterwards, I went for one at Mangan's, like I do on a Sunday.

The Rose of Tralee pageant was on with your man Pat Davis hosting because Gaybo's in hospital with colitis. Too many pub lunches and iffy egg mayonnaise, if you ask me. That fella would eat his own arm if you buttered it. So we're all watching the Aussie Rose sing "Waltzing Matilda" in a getup that looks like the drapes in the Wellington Court Hotel and Mary McGarry starts giving out to Tiny about didn't she see him one night chatting up a Brit with a tight jumper and buying her a Ritz, and wasn't it that same Brit Father Lenehan called the Angel of Death at Mass that very morning. So Tiny, who wasn't half a minute from buying his round, sits and takes it from her all the way through the Dublin Rose and the Boston Rose, and in the middle of the adverts he says, "At least I could get a word in edgewise with the girl," and out he goes. "Oh, Jaysus, I'm afflicted with the AIDS, sure I am," Mary starts in, so I took her next door to the chipper for a snack box and then we went back in just for a quick pint. The two of us were having a chat when who shows up but Nuala and tells me I was to get the dinner for the girls hours ago and I'm in desperate trouble.

All that night my stomach was very bad. Now a week's gone by and it's worse than ever. I had to drink the milk delivery this morning before it ever saw the inside of the icebox. Sure I'll catch hell from Nuala. Is it only sores you get when it's AIDS, or can it start in the stomach? Back in June after Ireland beat Italy in the World Cup, the craic was good and we were all up at Mangan's, the whole town it must have been, and Mary and I went 'round back, just for some air, and one thing led to another as it can. It was just a ride, I was sorry for it afterwards and took Nuala and her Aunt Molly with her feet so swollen she has to have them up all the time to the Wellington Court for dinner three Sundays in a row, but now my stomach's so bad I can't even manage a pint. And what if Tiny got it from the Brit and gave it to Mary and she gave it to me?

Father Brendan Lenehan

I never said the woman *intentionally* infected the lads she seduced. I gave the facts. All of this can be found in Deuteronomy 29:22, the stranger from a far land who brings plagues. This is my parish. If there is one among us who is the source of harm or evil, I am he who will, who *must,* spread the word. Have I any choice but to warn the people of this village of what travels in their midst? We are a small and by some standards sheltered nation. We do not know the dangerous ways of the world, our citizens know nothing of slayings on trains, the gays in their parades in wigs and bright frocks. This is a country where a lad can still hold a door open for a girl. We have no killers dressed as little old ladies lurking in the backseats of cars. These are people, you see, who must be warned of what dangers lie beyond the borders of Ireland. These are innocent people who will buy you a pint with their last pound and give you the shirts off their very backs.

I had her permission to speak at Mass on Sunday. She feels great remorse for what she has done, and has entrusted me to speak on her behalf. I will be the one to carry her message to all of Ireland.

Molly Hogan

All this week my legs have been a desperate red, with the pains through the middle of them. Jimmy hasn't been up to take out the rubbish or bring me my tablets. Useless is the word for Jimmy Faye when Nuala married him and useless is the word for him now. He's not a stable sort. It's a wandering eye he has, and he's been more on than off the dole as long as I've known him. Now Nuala's out working at Super Quinn six days a week, and all he has to do is get the little ones up and porridge for them in the morning.

I have lived in Ballymullet since I was a little girl. We moved here from Athboy before I could talk. I can remember when the IRA supporters would parade through the town and the shopkeepers closed down for the day. The people in this town have had a good dose of sympathy for the IRA. That is until now, when the young ones care more about the price of a pint than the dream of a united Ireland. Certainly no one's planning a hunger strike, unless you count my grandniece's craze with slimming pills. She's saving her money for a trip to a salon in Dublin where you can go for an artificial suntan. It's a sort of cooker you sit in—but only for a moment, or you'll be cooked inside as well as out. Can you imagine a girl with lovely Irish skin wanting a suntan? "Is it one of those colored girls you want to look like?" I asked her.

It's not the Ireland where I grew up anymore. My own children sleep through Sunday Mass, there's a vote on divorce next month, and the country is filling up with coloreds and Brits. My sister Rosie, in Galway, says you can't walk down the street without running into an Irish girl with a husband who's colored or British, sometimes both. I hear my grandchildren go on about coloring their hair purple—even the lads! And in the lounge at Mangan's I hear all manner of conversation about girls taking the ferry to England for a termination. Termination! Over pints they discuss terminations, as if it's the weather they're talking about. Do they think old women are deaf and blind?

Tiny McGarry

Two fellas came into Mangan's one afternoon hauling a cigarette machine, I thought it was, and lugged it into the corner beside the Gents. What do you know it's condoms they have for sale. You should have seen the look on the ladies' faces when they went for a pack of smokes. Jimmy Faye bought one, just for laughs, tossed it over to me, and said, "Where were these before Nollaig and Maureen?"—his fourth and fifth. Nollaig's a big girl, she likes a third helping whenever she can get it. It's not easy when you're on the dole and have five mouths to feed.

We're in for a quick one the Saturday following, and Tim Mangan and me are just after breaking up a row out back when what do we see but the same two fellas with the machine, this time in reverse.

"What's the idea, lads?" Tim Mangan says, "Business is booming!"

"We're on orders," the fella who looks to be in charge says.

Now Tim doesn't like the sound of this at all, because the machine's been a big draw all week. Everyone knows the pints are dear at Mangan's, a good 20p more than at the Priory or the Haggard Inn, but word got out, and everyone was coming into Mangan's for a look. You'd think Tim had put the Virgin Mary herself beside the Gents, and she was forgiving the wicked their trespasses.

They've been back once since, but a fella came in with a notice telling them to remove the machine from the premises before they even got it down the hall.

"Just set it down outside the chipper, next to the post box," I said. Everybody liked that one. Then Tim sees the fellas are serious about taking the machine back up to Dublin, and he starts shouting, if the British girls with social diseases are going to be taking their holidays in Ballymullet, then what we need is a condom machine in every pub in town. You'd think he was the priest himself, the way he's yelling about fire and brimstone and the great plague upon the city. Tommy MacIntyre over in his corner looks up from the *Independent* and says the famine already cut our numbers in half and how many each year gone to America for good on Donnelly visas, this country will empty out altogether if it's condoms we're using.

I'm thinking it must be a miracle if that Brit shagged eighty men in this town and has nothing to show for it. Our wives with the teething babbies screaming to wake the dead would wish their odds were half that good.

Mary McGarry

I heard that in America if you don't like your wife's jumpers, or say she's put on four stone since the day you married her, you can go to an office in the middle of town and ten minutes later you've your divorce papers in your hand, just like that. A friend of my sister's in Queens did that to his wife and then just disappeared, left her with three mouths to feed and she never saw or heard from him again. Now, here, that's not the way it is at all. You can have as many reasons as you've fingers on both hands, and I do, and you'll be getting the fella his dinner and ironing his work clothes 'til you're eighty, if he's even got steady work, which Tiny never does.

One night in April he came home from Mangan's full of drink, a bottle of Jameson's in his side pocket, and hit me square in the face when I wouldn't give him a ride. I didn't go out for days. I listen to Gerry Ryan on the radio every morning while I'm doing the washing and last week he was interviewing women with mean husbands.

I am sure Tiny was up to no good with that Brit. He's the sort, and he can blame me for not giving him a ride like a wife should. I didn't for three months, not since the night he hit me. I wrote the date on a slip of paper and each evening I marked down another day I'd kept him off me. Plenty of times I've passed Mangan's and seen him chattin' up one of the girls. I saw him with a girl after the Ireland-Italy match who I know was the Brit. She had that manky hair and dark pencil around the eyes, the way they wear it in London. I was blind that night—Jimmy Faye kept putting another bottle of Ritz in front of me, and there was port and brandies later when he said his stomach was gone and wouldn't take another pint.

The morning after the World Cup match I woke up and Tiny and I were beside each other in the bed without a stitch of clothing. I found my knickers on the floor and dressed before he woke and neither of us said a word about it. Ever since the night he hit me I have been sleeping in my flannels, except for that night.

I don't regret what I did with Jimmy Faye. He's a lovely man, couldn't hurt a woman if he tried, though his hands are big as hams and he had to steady himself against the door when we were out behind Mangan's. Now Father Lenehan says this Brit with AIDS has gone and given half the men in town a ride.

I am not up the pole, which is a good sign because I usually get pregnant when Tiny looks at me sideways. But if Tiny got a ride off the Brit that night, I've much more to worry about than a babby.

On my slip of paper I am still marking the days. I am not sure why.

Nollaig Faye

The first time I heard it was in the Boot, at the Friday disco. My cousin Ciaràn and his band were playing, so my mum said we could go. They know Nirvana and Green Day and Oasis, all the bands, they're brilliant. The bass player, Paddy Riordan, was the one who told me. It happened to a friend of his second cousin. His name is Brendan, but they call him Bunny. So Bunny was in the Banner Arms, out by the Dublin Road, after the hurling one Sunday, and there were a couple of Yanks there. Two girls, with rucksacks and tie-dye tee shirts.

"Where're you girls from?" he asks. From California, they say. Bunny gets chatting with the one of them, the lovely one— blonde hair, very slim, and she's drinking pints like she doesn't care that ladies drink glasses. They've just come over from Dublin, and they're looking for the nearest hostel. "The nearest one's in Donegal," Bunny tells them, which they'll never make by nightfall. The other girl gets talking to one of the Mangans, and this one takes a fancy to Bunny, and you know what American girls are like.

On the way out they pick up some Guinness at the off-license and head for home. The next morning Bunny wakes up and she's not in the bed with him. He goes into the Gents, and written on the mirror in bright red lipstick is "Welcome to the World of AIDS." Paddy says his second cousin told him no one's seen or heard from Bunny since. Anything could have happened. Some think he went up to Dublin and threw himself in the Liffey, but I don't know if I believe that.

Tina Johnston

To be honest, I wasn't even that crazy about going. I've always wanted to go to Greece or Hawaii, some sunny place. But my friend Denise's mother works for Calvin Klein, and Aer Lingus was running a promotion at one of her fashion shows. I won a drawing, and the prize was an all-expenses-paid trip to Ireland. The only thing I knew about Ireland was it rained all the time and everyone drinks a lot. Both of these things are true. But the guys are really nice, much nicer than American ones. In Dublin I met this one guy, and he wanted to bring me home to meet his parents. I said, "Look, we're in a *bar,* we're having a *drink.*" Some kind of big sports event that weekend, and everyone was walking around with scarves on and these little hats with pom-poms on the top. Everyone was hammered. Guys kept coming up to me and telling me I was beautiful and could they marry me. Not just guys my age, but old guys.

I let the one I met at the Harp, Ciaràn, take me back to the hotel where he was staying. It was cute because once he got my shirt off, he didn't know what to do. They talk like they know what's going on, but when it actually comes down to fooling around, they're lost. It's like they need a cigarette in one hand and a Guinness in the other or they lose their bearings. The only way those boys know how to use a tongue is to talk, which is just the opposite of American men.

This guy, he plays the drums. His specialty is the Irish one, which is called a bodhran. You don't pronounce the *d.* He tried to show me how to play it, but I couldn't get a rhythm going. Then he pulled out a bottle of whiskey, and we drank that for a while. I think he was pretty sure he was going to nail me. He had his fingers in my underwear and was feeling around, and I said, "Do you have a condom?"

He says no.

This part is priceless. "I always pull out," he says. "I've done it plenty of times and the girl has never gotten pregnant." "Is that so?" I say. Then I ask him if he's ever gotten a disease. "I'm an American," I say. I tell him I could have crabs. "Crabs?" he says, like I've told him I could have a horn growing out of my forehead. Then I tell him what Denise told me about her roommate Nicole's brother, who took a girl home from a bar in Valparaiso, and when he woke up in the morning the girl was gone. He didn't even know her last name. There was a note on his pillow that said, "Now you've got AIDS, sucker."

Of course that kind of put a damper on the evening, but I wanted to scare him. He was a nice kid, tall and shy with a good sense of humor and glasses that kept slipping down his nose. He was a good kisser, but you could tell he was not a seasoned professional. I was thinking, What if I sleep with this kid and he starts hanging out in bars like the Harp, scoping out American girls? He *could* end up with a disease someday. I'd feel bad if I didn't at least try to warn him, he seemed so clueless.

Ciaràn Faye

What's the worst chat-up line in Ireland?

"I'm from Ballymullet."

Brendan "Bunny" O'Hanlon

If I'm going to go looking for the craic at the weekend, Ballymullet is just where I pass through on the way to Donegal. Don't let anyone tell you the disco is worth it. As far as I can see, this AIDS scandal puts Ballymullet on the map. But allow me to make a logical point that seems to have been overlooked in the hysteria. If an English girl wanted to come to Ireland and infect a bunch of lads, what would she be doing in Ballymullet? I've been in the pubs at the weekend. Even at Mangan's all you see are the old fellas with their teeth as brown as the Guinness and day laborers trying to get away from their wives. I was there when Ireland beat Italy in the World Cup. I was bustin' for a pee, and the Gents was full, so I went out back and what do I see but these two old enough to be my mum and dad goin' for it up against a wall. They didn't even notice me.

Now I laugh whenever I turn on the TV and Father Lenehan is saying parents should tell their children to be responsible. Talk about the blind leading the blind. Besides, it's only the gay boys and drug pushers that get AIDS.

Tiny McGarry

They brought it back again. Tim got them to, and sure enough not five minutes after the boys installed it, Father Lenehan appeared like the Holy Spirit himself, with Molly Hogan on two legs that are only good for complaining about. Molly says they'll have an order for the removal of that purveyor of evil within twenty-four hours. Then she has the nerve to ask Tim Mangan for a pub lunch and a glass of Guinness and black currant, if you please. She sets herself up next to me and goes on about how if not for the generosity of Father Lenehan she'd perish in her sitting room waiting for Jimmy Faye to fetch her into town.

"What's next?" she asks. "Soon will Ballymullet be like Amsterdam, with the ladies selling themselves from behind glass?"

"I'm taking this action as part of a public health initiative," Tim Mangan says. The bollocks has got the lingo down so convincingly you'd think he was the chief executive of the Health Board himself.

Nollaig Faye

I looked lovely with my suntan, I did. Every mirror I passed I'd steal a glimpse of my new skin. In Grafton Street I bought a halter to show my shoulders, which had gone brown, not so pink as the rest of me. That night I went with Maureen and her mates to the clubs in Leeson Street. The fella who bought me the first drink was a Yank. His accent was brilliant. He said he played American football with a team in Saint Louie. In my purse I had a lipstick and the package I'd bought from the machine in Mangan's when no one was looking. The Abba song "Fernando" began playing, and he asked for a slow dance. Our pints were almost full, and he wanted to leave them on the ledge.

"If we leave them, someone will drink them," I said. He said that at decent clubs in America, no one stole your drink. "But this is Ireland," I said. We danced holding our pints over each other's shoulders, like the other couples. By the end of it, everyone had wet brown spots on their backs.

Then we were on a bed, and I didn't have my halter anymore, just my purse and my suntan. I'd had Ritz and cider and pints of Guinness I wouldn't touch at the Boot or Mangan's. I had the little package in my hand and then I didn't. "It's your first time, isn't it?" he said. I nodded in the dark. "You're safe your first time," he said.

It hurt. "Nothing's easy the first time," he said. In the morning he said he had a plane to catch and left. He left a key chain with the arch in Saint Louie on it for me. I met Maureen at the Bus Eireann station at nine, like we'd planned. We made up a story that Mum believed. I have nothing to worry about, but sometimes in the morning my stomach pains me. "You must have inherited the ulcers from your father," Mum says when he's within earshot. My suntan is starting to fade.

A Kind of Ireland

It had never seemed long or an island, with its strip malls that proliferated like infectious diseases, its tangle of clogged expressways that were not express ways of getting you anywhere, its obstinate drivers with their vanity plates and their cellular phones and their stereos playing at full throttle, all the distractae of a car culture. Coriander had always hated Long Island, that pushy Manhattan satellite, her homogenized homeland.

At the first chance she got she moved away, to Colorado. Her boyfriend, a macrobiotic chef who resented his Long Island upbringing for all the hours he'd spent sitting in traffic, wanted to ski. So they moved to Breckenridge, where they opened a vegetarian deli not far from the foot of a ski slope. Healthy Runs, they named it, not seeing until the words were painted on the deli's plate glass window what an unfortunate oxymoron they'd invented, what a bad jab at bowels. But people in Breckenridge were forgiving—in a town devoted entirely to facilitating the transport of people outfitted in neon Gore-Tex and oversized polyurethane slats up and down colossal hills, people were willing to forgive all kinds of indulgences. Being named after a spice did not seem the least bit quaint or ridiculous in a town where the mock-Victorian townhouses, painted pastel blues and yellows and pinks, were trimmed with curlicue-covered shutters that made them look like the prototype for Candyland. Even giving a macrobiotic deli a name that gestured in the direction of bowel dysfunction could be indulged in a town like this.

Anything could be indulged here, it seemed. But then Kip took a skiing lesson. That put a kink in the plans.

"I can't work days," he told Coriander. "I need to ski."

But everyone *else* in Breckenridge needed to ski. The whole point, Coriander tried patiently to explain, was that all Breckenridgians wanted so obsessively to ski that they were willing to pay her and Kip outrageous amounts of money for beige grains and fermented soy. Outrageously expensive beige grains and soy would give the skiers energy to hassle in lift lines and barrel down giant hills in their neon Gore-Tex.

For a while, Kip came in and made deli salads at night. During the day, Coriander soaked the quinoa and the seaweed, pressure-cooked the chickpeas, rinsed the seitan. She had always wanted to be a chef, but cooking for so many skiers and asking them to fork over so much money for her mediocre creations made her nervous. The uncooked ingredients never looked anything like the finished product. Millet and amaranth resembled nothing so much as birdseed; red lentils turned green when cooked. Tempeh had a curious smell and gray spots that looked like mold, though words on the package assured that this was natural. Coriander had always wanted to learn how to cook a big, elegant meal, to make things with scalloped edges, to julienne, to puree. But she had never gotten beyond boiling things for Kip.

She tried to teach herself how to do more than boil things.

Kip, meanwhile, was learning how to ski moguls.

When Healthy Runs folded, Kip shrugged. He was staring out the window of the pink mock-Victorian he and Coriander shared with four underage trust-funders from Connecticut. In the sunlight the mountains looked to her like spun sugar, a giant whipped confection, something that would snatch your loyalties from lentils and rice.

Sugar had always given her the blues.

Of all the holidays, Coriander had always loved Halloween best. She would gorge on candy until her blood raged through her, a sugary stew. She became short-tempered and weepy, her adrenals finally giving up, giving out, and one day she'd go to dip into her stash and it would be gone. Her mother would have dumped it, the whole mood-altering mound of it.

Was it any wonder she'd fallen for a man who could manage to make a tasty meal of kale and a yam?

She drove back to Long Island in her Plymouth Horizon. She drove back without Kip. But just to have something to remember him by, she took with her some of his stainless steel pressure cookers and steamers, his woks and sharp knives. There were moments during the four days of speeding eastbound along Route 80 when the tools of Kip's trade clanked and rattled against each other, a reminder of her sentimental theft. She had never imagined herself as sentimental or thieving. But then, she had never imagined herself as a failed small business owner dumped by a macrobiotic skiing fanatic, either.

❖❖❖

Her parents didn't lecture her about her lack of business acumen; there had never been any illusion that she had any. But the boyfriend—couldn't she have predicted that he would waltz off to the top of the first tall peak?

"Kip was no more reliable than a hormone," said her mother, who was muddling her way through menopause and had a bone to pick with hormones. Hormones, it seemed, were responsible for her mother's new hairstyle and color, boyishly short and black as shoe polish. Also for a new wardrobe that featured flowing violet tunic shirts and matching slacks. She showed Coriander into her old bedroom, redone in purple and gold.

There were paintings of goddesses and rainbows on the walls. "I know it doesn't look like the room you remember," she said. "But you can stay as long as you want." Then her mother sighed. "They just take over," she said, as if hormones weren't biochemistry but invisible and highly persuasive fashion consultants and hairstylists and upholsterers.

It was clear that her mother liked the idea of having her back in the nest again. Such an arrangement implied that motherhood was not a job in a temp agency, that menopause was not God's booby prize for child rearing.

❖❖❖

Coriander was twenty-eight years old and in debt and back under her parents' roof. None of this bothered her as much as living on Long Island again. Driving in bumper-to-bumper traffic to work at Food for Thought, she began feeling like a lion she had once seen on a nature show. A pack of hyenas had surrounded the lion, isolating it from the others. The hyenas began attacking the lion, each one leaping and biting or swiping at it. There was a stylized, theatrical kind of circling and an eerie cackling. The narrator of the movie set up the hyenas as a filthy bunch of street kids, muggers out for a joyride. The lion was the nine-to-fiver just trying to make a living.

After a few months at home, she began cutting in front of feebler customers at the bagel shop. She steered through the parking lot at the Roosevelt Field Mall with a kind of flushed, angry fervor. When someone called to peddle a *Newsday* subscription, she sang an epithet and hung up the phone.

"You seem to be adjusting," her mother said. Her mother was not adjusting, not to the hot flashes and the weight gain, not to the swing and dip of her moods.

"I'm not adjusting, Mom," said Coriander. "I'm numb."

❖❖❖

Coriander's father went to New Jersey overnight for a software expo. Her mother invited a woman named Joetta over for shrimp parmesan.

"Joetta's the one who took care of me during that whole ordeal with my ankle," her mother said. *Ordeal* was a favorite word of her mother's. But the ankle really had been an ordeal. She had broken it while playing racquetball, and Joetta, who worked in the shipping department of the mail-order company where Coriander's mother was a customer service representative, had appointed herself caretaker.

At six o'clock a woman in a Mets sweatshirt and white high-top sneakers came to the door. She had short, graying hair and wire-rimmed glasses with lenses tinted a green that made Coriander think of algae.

"You're Joetta?" Coriander said. She had been expecting someone southern and petite, with a drawl.

"I'm early," Joetta said, and stepped inside. "You look just like her!" she cried, hugging Coriander.

At dinner Joetta wanted to hear all about Coriander's life: what Colorado had been like, how her new job at the food co-op was going, if she still resented Kip, whether she had met anyone new.

"Actually, I have," said Coriander. She was on her second glass of white zinfandel and had forgotten that her mother might not like the idea of the man she had started seeing. He was an Irishman, which was not the problem. The problem was that he was divorced and had a five-year-old daughter. All this she blurted out before remembering that she had meant to omit certain details.

"This guy doesn't sound a whole lot better than Kip the skiing fool," Joetta said. "Is your picker broken?" She lifted a piece of shrimp off her plate and bit it, then put the forlorn little pink tail down in front of Coriander.

"That's for sure," Coriander's mother said. She was still picking at some tomato wedges and did not look up.

❖ ❖ ❖

One night when Joetta came for dinner there was an ice storm. The rain that had been coming down all day turned shimmery and treacherous on the ground. Even die-hard Long Islanders, with their unwavering faith in the ability of their snazzy cars to get them anywhere, stayed off the roads.

Coriander was sitting on her bed and staring at a cylindrical bayberry candle the size of a roll of toilet paper. "Joe's going to stay here tonight, okay?" her mother said.

Later that evening, Coriander went up to her mother's bathroom to look for some Q-tips. There was a waxy buildup in her ears, she was convinced, that was causing her to miss things.

Her mother's bathroom had a sliding door connecting it to her bedroom. It was open just enough for Coriander to peek through and see Joetta sitting on her father's side of the bed. She had the remote control in one hand and Coriander's mother's foot in the other. "That feels great," her mother was saying. Joetta was changing the channel and massaging the foot. She was under the covers on Coriander's father's side of the bed, and he was at a software expo in New Jersey. Probably he was drinking Manhattans with his boss in the bar of some overpriced hotel. Her father's boss drank too much, and her father, a passive and agreeable man, usually tried to keep up with him.

Coriander went back downstairs, blew out her bayberry candle, and climbed into bed. She thought about her father with his too-long string of drinks (Cape Codder, Manhattan, and, of course, Long Island iced tea, with its frenetic mishmash of rums and whiskeys, rush hour in a glass) and her mother sitting in bed with her foot in Joetta's hand.

❖ ❖ ❖

She started spending more time at the Irishman's. His name was Seamus, a name she had never believed belonged to a real person. It was like someone from Switzerland being named Heidi.

Seamus worked at the gourmet deli next door to the food co-op. He would dash through the co-op on his way to make a delivery of buttermilk scones to a mansion in Cold Spring Harbor, or seven punch bowls and a block of ice shaped to look like a bag of golf clubs. He was the one his boss preferred for deliveries; Americans favored anyone with an accent that sounded vaguely British.

"Vaguely British!" Seamus scoffed at Coriander. "I'm no more British than you are!"

"We're a nation of Anglophiles." Coriander sighed. She was as susceptible as anyone else to such accents, and partial to the dent in Seamus's chin as well.

Seamus lived in a tiny cottage in Sea Cliff with two roommates, an Englishman and a Welshman, both working in the country illegally. The Welshman worked construction, the Englishman tended bar just down the road, at the Dribble Inn. Coriander began going to the Dribble in the evenings with Seamus and William, the Welshman. It was a hole-in-the-wall, really, with a scarred pool table and bar stools with plastic cushions, but they served Guinness and Bass on tap, and all the bartenders had those accents, the swerving musical lilts of people who had learned the language on the other side of the Atlantic. The Englishman, Martin, always said, "Drink up, lads!" when he served them their beers.

For all the trouble these people had taken to get to America, and for all the hoopla they made about what a great country this was, there seemed to be a concerted effort to make the Dribble seem like the kind of pub they had left behind. The TV was always tuned to a cable channel that broadcast British and Irish sports, old men and young sat side by side and bought each other rounds, and all of them smoked continuously and unapologetically, as if the news about lung cancer had never reached them. The Budweiser, pale and fizzy as seltzer, bland as an American accent, was served in pint glasses. It was never quite cold enough.

"You're in construction?" Coriander asked William while Seamus was getting pints for them. "What is it you construct?"

"I tear down gas stations and put up new ones," he said.

His bulk did seem to be the type that people got from ripping things apart. "Is that what you did back in Wales?"

"I lost my job back in Wales."

"You were white-collar there, I bet."

"You're psychic, are you, Coriander?"

"I once heard you quoting Nietzsche on the phone."

"Even we working-class blokes can memorize, if you give us a good mnemonic device."

"That's not what I meant," Coriander said.

"I know, luv." He grinned and pattered out a rhythm on her knees with his palms.

Seamus came back and put a pint of Guinness in front of Coriander. For himself and William he had pints of Budweiser. Seamus called Guinness a big filthy pint and winced at it as if it were varnish. Guinness was opaque and stubborn, a pint that took forever to pull. The bartender had to pour part of it and then let it sit before filling the glass to the rim.

"We were talking about my previous incarnation as a respectable white-collar type," William said.

"Ah," said Seamus. "Coming to this country was a step down for your man Will. Luckily, I didn't have that problem."

"A lateral move for Seamus."

Seamus took a giant gulp of his beer. "Worked for Super Quinn. I was a stocker."

A snappy name, even if it was a grocery store. Better than King Soopers, the supermarket near Coriander's house when she lived in Colorado. She imagined Seamus lining up jars of herring, boxes of oats, bags of boiled sweets.

Boiled sweets. That's what they called hard candies in Ireland. There was something sexual about boiled sweets. She hadn't slept with Seamus yet, but she was planning on it. *You're grand,* she imagined him saying, *my boiled sweet.*

❖❖❖

Seamus had a narrow bed for himself and another, a trundle bed that his daughter used when she stayed with him. Sometimes when Coriander showed up, the trundle bed was still out. There was something upsetting about licking Seamus's neck in a room where his daughter slept. The reminders Coriander stumbled across seemed oddly sinister: Barbie's platinum hair (where had the newly bald Barbie gone? why had the daughter shorn her of her hair?), a book called *Favorite Bible Stories* (when watered down and fed to children, Bible stories always chilled Coriander), a pencil drawing of a cat surrounded by what looked like fire.

There were only two bedrooms. William slept on the couch.

"How do you manage?" Coriander asked. She could not see how people could live so precariously, how they could leave their homes and families and the acres of green untouched land and fly to America and settle on Long Island, this morass of malls, this clot in the neck of the Northeast.

"We're a resourceful bunch of bastards," William said. He was building a drafting table in the living room. In Wales he'd been an architect.

Seamus was setting up a CD player he'd bought. "Come look, Cori," he called from his bedroom.

Propped up on the dresser were several close-up color photos of a mouth. "The oral surgeon's takin' me for everything I'm worth," he said. "But once I'm done with that nonsense I'll be able to complete my entertainment center."

"What's it going to cost you?"

Seamus squinted. "I'd say in the neighborhood of eight grand."

Coriander looked around at the contents of his room: the bed with its trundle bed tucked underneath, the CD player teetering on a milk crate, four bare walls, the photos of his gray and unpretty teeth.

"The Irish have never had much enthusiasm for dental hygiene," said Seamus. "We prefer soccer."

❖❖❖

Back home, Coriander's parents were making vacation plans.

"Your father wants to sail around the Caribbean on a catamaran," her mother said. "I'm looking for the Landlubber's Special. Give me your tired, your weary, your rum punchless . . ."

"Why can't you compromise and do half land, half sea?" Coriander asked.

"Don't make a scene out of this," her mother said. There were ordeals and there were scenes.

Coriander felt something throb in her neck. "Don't tell me Joetta's coming along,"

"Okay, I won't."

"She is?"

"I'm not going to take my one vacation of the year alone, Coriander." She was trying on all her bathing suits and scrutinizing herself in the mirror.

"What does she look like in a bathing suit, I wonder?" Coriander said. She pictured Joetta in a black-and-white striped one, loping toward a chaise lounge.

"Don't be cruel," said her mother. "Don't be a bitch."

Her mother had never used that word with her before. It stung like a slap. She went downstairs and picked around in the pantry until she found a hidden box of Mallomars, then ate six.

❖❖❖

"My parents are taking separate vacations," she told Seamus. They were at the Dribble, watching the World Cup trials live from Ireland. Northern Ireland was playing the Republic.

"Good for them," Seamus said. "A couple that vacations separately stays together. Maybe Rosemary and I should have tried that."

"You think it's okay for them to take separate vacations?"

"Look, honey," said Seamus. "I barely made it through three years. If they're goin' on thirty they must be doing something right."

"They're just putting in their time."

"That's what marriage is, horse." He called her that sometimes. It surprised her that he would choose such a homely term of endearment. Maybe he was so used to being a husband that he had forgotten about those other words—sweetie, baby, darling, doll.

Seamus put his arm around her and kissed her ear. A roar went up in the bar. "We're goin', Cori!" he shouted. He kissed her again, then joined a group of men who were leaping up and down and singing a song about how they were all a part of Jackie's army and would really shake 'em up when they won the World Cup.

You're not going anywhere, Coriander thought. And neither am I. She stared out the window at the Stationhouse Cafe, a grubby little diner that stood beside the train tracks and the mini mall. It was always the same lineup: 7-Eleven, colossal drugstore, laundromat, liquor store, pizza place, video store. You could drive along the main road of any town around here and it would look almost exactly like the main road of any other town. There were gas stations at every intersection, and more popping up all the time, like canker sores. Long Island was drowning in convenience. It was like cutting off your nose because that made it more convenient to pull your shirt over your head. But what about the nose? Didn't the nose deserve an advocate?

She stayed out all day with Seamus. By dinnertime she was drunk. He took her back to the cottage and made them scrambled eggs with ketchup. They ate on his bed, Seamus sitting back against the pillows and Coriander in the V of his legs.

She was happy here.

"I would kill for some rashers," Seamus said and shook some ketchup on a slice of bread.

She thought she would like to live in a place like that, a place where people called their food boiled sweets, black pudding, rashers. There was something raw and unforgiving about rashers. It was not at all like benign bacon, it did not attempt to deny a pig the horror of its death.

The phone rang, and Seamus hopped up to get it. After a few minutes Coriander wandered into the living room, where William and Martin were watching a cooking show. Coriander thought of Kip and his yams. She hoped he'd skied above his ability and broken something.

"It's his ex," Martin said.

Coriander sidled up against the wall and tried to listen.

"About the spirit that's been following me around?" Seamus was saying. "Well, you can ask her."

When he hung up the phone, Coriander followed him back into his bedroom. "What spirit that's been following you around?"

"Ah, well," he said, and cleared his throat.

"Tell me."

"It's nothing," he said. "You wouldn't understand."

"I would," she pleaded, though she wasn't sure this was true. She already knew he was going to tell her something mystical and metaphysical, something completely inconsistent with the geometric grid of her logic. Perhaps he was right, perhaps the monotony of malls had already been bred too much into her bones.

"There's a woman at work who says she sees a spirit following me. She's a good spirit, she's watching over me. She has sort of rust-colored hair and she wants to remind me to have a hot breakfast in the morning. Recently I've just been having jam and bread." Seamus took his pants off and climbed into bed. "That was Rosemary on the phone. She wants me to call my mother in Ireland and find out what color my grandmother's hair was."

Coriander took off her own pants and climbed into bed.

"Those are lovely panties you have," said Seamus. "Well, you see, I'm not sure I want to ask my mother because we're a very superstitious family." He began taking off her panties.

"I see," said Coriander, though she didn't really see. She

pictured Seamus's family, the whole Irish Catholic lot of them, with their brogues and their beliefs in fairies and their admonitions from spirits to eat good breakfasts. She pictured them in a quaint village like the ones re-created for American theme parks, no malls for miles, maybe no malls at all.

"Don't you miss Ireland?" she asked.

"I'm here now," he said cheerfully.

But when they went to the Dribble after one of his soccer practices and she saw how he and the other players bought each other rounds, how they laughed and drank their pints and slagged each other—that was what they called it, slagging—it was clear that they missed their country.

Coriander wished she had a spirit following her around. Or that she was capable of believing in a spirit following her around. What she needed was an ounce of superstition, a teaspoonful, a milligram. She remembered Seamus telling her about his mother, who carried a tiny vial of holy water in the glove compartment of her car to prevent car accidents.

"Seamus?" she whispered. He had already begun to snore in her ear, another discomfort of two of them trying to sleep in a narrow bed made for one. "Could we pull out the trundle bed?"

He pulled out the bed underneath his, the one his daughter used when she stayed there, and Coriander climbed into it. But it sat several inches lower than Seamus's bed did; she couldn't put her arms around him without cutting off her circulation. She had to settle for laying one of her hands over one of his.

❖ ❖ ❖

Early one morning she came home from Seamus's with a hangover and went straight into the shower. I overslept, she was planning to tell her mother. Seamus had gotten up at 5 A.M. and put on a Nat King Cole Christmas CD, and they had made love on his floor to "O Come, All Ye Faithful." It was deep December:

time to get festive, time to shop. Time, Coriander had said, to kill yourself if the days didn't stop getting shorter.

She stood in the shower and let the water soak her in great, pulsing waves. After a few moments she found herself holding a big block of soap, sweet smelling and flecked with oats. She had bought it thinking Seamus would like a woman who smelled like cooked cereal.

When she got out of the shower, her mother was waiting in the hallway. "You've been drinking."

"Not merely drinking." Coriander held a hand in the air with her index finger pointed toward the ceiling. She went into her bedroom, flung her towel on her bed, and began to look for something to wear to work. "Marinating."

Her mother came into her bedroom and sat on the bed. "I don't know what's happened to you since the Colorado thing fell through. Sleeping with someone who is obviously a drunk, who works in a deli . . . "

It was clear that *deli* was the worst of it.

"Mom," Coriander said, "*I'm* a drunk who works in a deli."

"It's not a deli."

"A glorified grocery store. I'm going in early this morning because we're getting a delivery. I open the boxes and put price stickers on all the items with a little plastic gun. Then I put things on the shelves. I'm a stock girl."

Her mother harrumphed. "You do other things."

"Sometimes I work the cash register. Sometimes I walk around and help customers find things. Sometimes we walk around and never find the thing the customer is looking for."

"Your life . . . ," her mother said. "If I were you I'd start thinking hard about how to jump-start it."

Coriander put on a pair of jeans and a sweatshirt that Seamus had given her. It had a picture of a soccer ball surrounded by shamrocks and the slogan *All the Way to Italia!* printed on it. People in Ireland were mortgaging their houses for World Cup tickets. People were playing the lottery instead of buying groceries.

At the top of the stairs there was a suitcase open on the floor with her mother's bathing suits in it, all five of them. The bed was neat and untouched on her father's side.

Her mother saw her and held up a hand. "He's all wrong for you," she said.

"He's not wrong, he's just different than the ones I usually go for."

Her mother opened the drawer of her night table and took out a bottle of pills and a new estrogen patch. "He's out for one thing."

"That's Joetta talking. You never used to talk to me like that."

"You never used to get involved with these types. I know these types."

"What types do you mean?" Something fierce and bitter was building in her. Too much sugar, she thought, remembering her pints of Guinness, her forays into Mallomars. Alcohol was really just sugar, fermented anger. Something was going to fizz over, like a carbonated beverage, shaken. "What do you mean, these types? That he's poor? That he's divorced?" She could hear herself getting shrill. "That he's a man?" she shouted. "Could the problem be that he happens to be a man?"

Her mother paused in the middle of the room. She was still holding the bottle of pills in one hand and the patch in the other. The pills were supposed to keep her thyroid from shutting down entirely; the estrogen patch was supposed to prevent her insides from shriveling.

"I don't hate men," her mother said. She sat down on the bed and began to cry. "I don't hate them. I don't know why you had to say that."

Coriander went over and sat down next to her.

"I'm fifty years old, Coriander," her mother whispered. "I don't even recognize this body anymore. I don't recognize your father. Do you understand? You don't understand yet."

"No," said Coriander. Her body felt sturdy and reliable around her bones, efficient as a beehive. It was not yet shriveling, or ballooning, or in any other way betraying her. She thought of Seamus handing her a pint in the Dribble, his hand tickling her back while they watched Gaelic football on TV, the two of them tangled in a sleeping bag on Seamus's bedroom floor, him sighing, *Ah you're lovely, you are,* as if Coriander were some fine and exotic species, part familiar, part mysterious.

Coriander fit her face into the crook of her mother's neck, her first comfort on Earth. It smelled pleasantly familiar, this neck, though it did not smell quite like she remembered her mother smelling. Later she would identify the smell as men's cologne, a spicy commercial musk a college boyfriend had worn. This mother of hers, with all her pleasantly familiar parts and smells, was no longer the home of Coriander's infancy. Her mother might have the same name, but there had been a significant rearrangement while she, Coriander, was away with Kip in Colorado.

And then Coriander had come home alone to this new mother and this same old Long Island and to Seamus. So she had turned Long Island into a different island, a kind of Ireland, a place where people held up under misfortune, where misfortune went out and had a beer. A place where people looked forward to pints and boiled sweets and maybe some cod and chips in a paper bag. But not further forward than that.

"When your world isn't working, you invent one," her mother said, this mother who had invented her.

"Yes," said Coriander, thinking of Seamus's daughter and her bald Barbie, of Seamus eating his oatmeal at the behest of his auburn-haired guardian spirit, of his whole family and their legions of concerned spirits, real or imagined. And then she thought of Joetta massaging her mother's foot.

Something in her heart stumbled and fell.

She saw herself as a baby in the apartment in Oyster Bay where her parents had lived when she was born, exit 41 off the Expressway. She saw her parents sealing off the kitchen and filling it with steam so the room would be warm when she had her bath. They had bathed her in the kitchen sink, holding her head the way they had learned in new parents' class.

Something in her heart stumbled and fell and got up again, a ski lesson of the spirit.

"You try to have someone watch out for you," she said.

"Yes," her mother said. "It's the only way to survive at all."

Opposites

The changing room at Jones Beach is filled with mothers and babies, long wooden benches, cement floors dotted with clumps of wet toilet paper, dripping showerheads, diapers soiled and clean, pale light that filters through the plastic roof, wet heat, sounds of mothers that aren't words. My bathing suit is all black. Yours has bunches of balloons. You stand in the middle of the room and stare.

In the ocean I hold you over the waves. We spit seawater at each other, you through the gap made by your lost tooth. He crashes out past the breakwater and gets knocked over. In the shallows you show us you can be a blowfish, starfish, mean fish, up-leg fish. Your head underwater, leg in the air, his arms on my waist, tongue salty in my mouth. Then you're up for a breath.

I saw you kiss.

That's right, doc, he says. He lifts you high in the air so when I look up it's just you and the sky.

❖ ❖ ❖

Some nights all three of us stay in the room he rents, you away from your mother Tuesdays and Fridays, me away from mine any night I can. I never meant to have to move back home, but there's no need to tell you that sad story. Six and living back and forth between your parents, you have enough story of your own. It matters only to me that I had one bedroom growing up, with bookshelves and a canopy bed and a dust ruffle and yellow light and cats. You have this trundle bed in the room he rents and the middle drawer in his dresser for your clothes and toys.

The nights we both stay here, he gets up for his shower without saying anything. *Good morning, Patrick,* I say as he leaves the room. In your sheets on the trundle bed you click another loose tooth with your tongue.

Do you not say anything to each other in the morning?

He teached me to be like that.

❖ ❖ ❖

I like driving his van. It's high up and airy, a moving hallway. When he drives, we both sit in the passenger seat, you in my lap. It's not safe. We examine each other's palms and eyes with a magnifying glass. There is a powdery new smell always in your hair.

Happy.

Sad.

Healthy.

Sick.

Girl.

Boy.

Hope.

No hope?

We like this game, Opposites. No hope, I say, is also Despair.

❖ ❖ ❖

In Manhattan I thought I was going to have to tell him I lost you. Amid the pink hive of dolls and girls I could see Bridal Barbie, her gown lit by a lightbulb underneath. Aerobics Barbie leaping on her impossible tiptoes. In the center of the room, life-sized Barbie, my prettier mirror, though all her sayings were canned.

Ballroom Barbie was where I found you, waltzing to the water fountain. He had left for a pretzel from the vendor outside.

In the train on the way home we had a Cinderella coin bank, the bottom of her bell-shaped dress a trap door that opened with a plastic key. We had corn chips in a shiny orange sack. The key wouldn't turn in the bank and broke. *So you have my luck with money,* Patrick said. I unbent a paper clip and yanked her dress open. Inside were a purple barrette, flower earrings, a tiny useless pink comb. In went the chips. Our hands got greasy quick.

The man in front of us wore a red shirt with a sheen and a black veil.

He's sad, you said. The man turned. It felt like he wanted to tell us everything. He was on his way from a ceremony. In Chelsea. For his lover. He tripped over these details, delivered them staccato. I said, in the manner of adults, *I'm sorry.* You asked for the veil and he gave it. You posed, flirting: *I'm lovely. I am.*

You are.

You try.

I sat the black netting over my eyes and the man held his hands up and clicked one finger against the air.

Now me. No, with the veil. I'm the bride.

Take it, the man said when he got up to leave. *Tomorrow I'm going to buy something velvet.*

So we traded and gave him our purple barrette and flower earrings and tiny useless pink comb.

❖ ❖ ❖

I only drive when he isn't with us, at work or the gym. We play the game with the steering wheel. I quick-swivel it and we yell through the curves. The van, being big, only swerves a little.

Big.

Little.

Love.

Hate.

Pineapple.

Pineapple doesn't have an opposite.

We buy a pineapple. The spikes are prickly, and when we eat too much our tongues sing with acid.

❖ ❖ ❖

Hot Sundays in August we go to the pool at the Y. He likes to sit on the edge and read the *Irish Echo*. You like when I walk along the diving board and pluck at the air, picking imaginary daisies. Then wander off and topple headlong. Belted in your Styrofoam bubble, you leap in and save me. One of his hands drags in the water. The next time he waves, his fingertips are black with newsprint.

He goes in for dips, never swims. When you grab for him, he turns and kicks up a foamy wake. For dinner we have tuna and ketchup sandwiches and cans of root beer. You drop yours, shrieking, and we catch the froth on the floor with our hands.

❖ ❖ ❖

At Christmas he gives me a bottle of Emmett's Irish whiskey and two small goblets. We wait in the landlord's living room for you to fall asleep.

On the couch he and I lounge and kiss, lazy against each other as shadows in summer. We peel an orange, and my hands sting where I have chewed my fingertips. On the bedroom floor we cover ourselves with a sheet and move together. Above me in your bed you whisper in your sleep.

In the night you wake me and ask if there are ghosts.

There are no such things as ghosts.

He got you a ring.

I tell you to stop playing fibs and go to sleep.

In the night he runs his tongue down my back until I shiver. I ask him if there are ghosts.

Not in this country, he says. This country is still too young.

❖ ❖ ❖

In the west of Ireland the sheep that dot the hills are marked on their backs with blue or red dye. The fur is not called wool until they shear it off. In Ireland when you drive around a bend a statue of the blessed Virgin blooms by the side of the road, a blurred white blot.

I worry that you won't remember my face.

Water, I think.

Alive.

Veil.

❖ ❖ ❖

This is what he tells me:

In Clonakilty there was a woman all in white at the bottom of a well. When they turned her over, the back of her dress was soaked with blood. Once a year at daybreak the doors of the houses open and all the women come out wearing white.

In the morning you turn in my arms and ask why there was blood on her dress.

❖ ❖ ❖

The night before I get in my car to drive across eight states he drinks pint after pint. We sit at the bar among the soccer players from the technical institute down the road. Late in the evening he leans on me, slurring and smoking.

They're going somewhere, he tells me. *So are you.*

I tell him he can go somewhere. He can come with me.

But he's an eejit, he says.

And he has you.

It always comes to this.

I am the one who drives the van home. Up high, my feet squeaking in new sandals, I like the van even better when I am drunk. By the time we turn onto Northern Boulevard he is snoring. On the parkway I quick-swivel the steering wheel and whisper *Whoa Whoa Whoa* on the curves.

❖ ❖ ❖

Before I leave for Utah, we take you to the House of Pancakes, to sweeten it with syrup. You say you're getting a stack blue with berries. But when I order chicken soup and tuna salad so do you.

We sit beside each other in the booth and break saltines onto our bread plates. The maze on the children's menu goes unwandered with the crayons the waitress brings in a cup. Instead you pummel me, your knuckles knocking against my ribs.

Why can't she go to school here? I love you. I hate you.

Behave, he says.

Misbehave.

Don't get cheeky with me, Missy.

❖ ❖ ❖

In the van on the way to drop you off at your mother's house I hold you and say *Hello.*

Good-bye.

Near.

Far.

When the screen door has closed and you are waving to me behind it, I see how I should have said *Far* and let you end with *Near.* Every pair has a right order and a wrong.

❖ ❖ ❖

Pennsylvania, Ohio, half of Indiana, the windshield smeared gray with insects. On postcards there isn't room to write much of anything. I send one per rest stop and say a lot of nothing. What is the opposite of cornfield? How can I draw you this endless American sky?

In Nebraska there are box elder bugs on the motel pillow. I flick them away and pretend not to see where they land. I chose this Econo Lodge because of the pool. At night I go and hold my breath underwater for a minute, then two. There is no fun in a tea party alone, no one to lift a cup to, pinkie out.

Across Wyoming I play my tape deck all the way. I sing, but softly. There is a lot of land here, little water.

Alive, I once said, and you said *Drowned.*

Pregnancy Scares

The male pursues the female for the purpose of sexual union.
—Sigmund Freud

Just hold the absorbent tip in your urine stream for a few seconds.
—Clearblue Easy Early Pregnancy Test instructions

Meg was pregnant. She hadn't done the test yet, but she felt off kilter: something had hatched in her. She ducked out of work early and walked to the Rite Aid near Grand Central and stood, stranded and mournful, in the feminine hygiene aisle. Products with names that managed to gesture coyly toward and away from the part of the anatomy in question surrounded her—the Vagi-Gard and the Vagicaine and the Vaginex. Then the Answer One Step Ovulation Prediction Test, the Astroglide Personal Lubricant. The Femstat, the Monistat, the this and that -stat, a bevy of remedies for what seemed to be a late twentieth-century glut in yeast production, everything boxed in pinkish florals. Feminine hygiene as prissy science. The Gyne-Lotrimin. The Gynecort: feminine hygiene as gated community: "Discover Relaxed Country Living at the Gynecort!"

❖ ❖ ❖

She hadn't bought a pregnancy test since her twenties (her twenties! could she really be old enough, at thirty-three, to speak of her life in decade-long chunks?). As the days without any sign of a period began to add up, the Boyfriend would grow more flatly reassuring in proportion to her mounting hysteria. For someone who described her political leanings as "almost communist," her thoughts always seemed to slip out of her cellophane-wrapped in the language of commerce: *Mounting Hysteria—now available in Decade-Long Chunks!* Not since the pre-AIDS-anxiety days of the early eighties had she skulked into a pharmacy and tried to fake the breeziness of someone buying a box of Kleenex. Back in her twenties, she would try to neutralize the effect by grouping the pregnancy test in with neutral items she grabbed off the shelves in foggy panic: antifungal foot powder, wart remover, Darth Vader Pez dispensers. Only later, when the pregnancy test had informed her that she was still the only one living in her body, was she able to survey her choices: her feet didn't have fungus, she needed no warts removed, the Pez dispensers she gave to a neighbor's kids.

She comparison-shopped pregnancy tests, weightless and rattling, racy versions of tiddlywinks, life's wicked little parlor game for women. Rows of them in their postconsumer packaging, pink and blue and hopeful. They favored adjectives and verbs: *Precise. Conceive. Confirm. Confirm*'s gimmick alone made her nauseated—in lieu of the plain old blue and pink to purple lines on a strip, your positive result showed up inside a little picture of a heart. "Your results can be saved in a memorable keepsake card for your baby's book. To save your result, follow insert instructions." But she and the Boyfriend had already botched, so to speak, the insert instructions. As if 97 percent of people who bought the tests weren't practically crapping in their pants about the prospect of pregnancy. As if women were just rushing out to make sure they'd gotten knocked up after their mistaken trysts on New Year's Eve, at their high school reunions, at their best friends' weddings. You would think, in this techno-logical age, that there would be something more honest about pregnancy tests, something more, as the marketers liked to put it, user-friendly.

She pictured herself breaking the news to the Boyfriend. There would be a plate of linguini, the Boyfriend's favorite food. Her on one side of the table, the Boyfriend on the other. Between them, linguini. A conversation. Garlic bread? She couldn't plan any further than the linguini. The Boyfriend also liked beer in the can and televised sporting events, and he liked it when Meg wore thong underwear. The thong underwear made her feel like a turkey, its soon-to-be-fought-over drumsticks tied up with string in preparation for a long siesta in an oven. The main difference between Meg in a thong and the turkey in string was that the turkey was dead, a fact that, from a neurological perspective, gave the turkey a clear advantage.

"The predicament of possible progeny," Meg said to herself in the Rite Aid aisle, then hoped she hadn't been overheard and taken for a crazy person. Alliterating always made her feel better, the way a vodka Collins made some people feel better. She needed a little cerebral anesthesia. It was the coy science of it all that she hated, the miniature pipettes and test tubes, the powder or litmus strip that turned pink or got a bull's-eye in the center of it if you were pregnant:

> *If you see a blue control line and a pink to purple test line, you are pregnant.*
> *If you see only a blue control line and no pink to purple test line, you are probably not pregnant.*

These were the instructions on the back of a box that had the words *Unmistakable +/- result!* on the front. *Probably not.* Here your life was, ready to split; here your body was, maybe doubling already, and you were expected to be making a judgment call about a litmus strip.

You "performed" a pregnancy test. Like a monologue, or a sex act. All over America they were being performed: in employee bathrooms, in the middle of blizzards, in shorts and tee shirts on

cross-country trips, in panic and near hysteria, in cahoots, in
Connecticut, in December, in despair. Most of what women
learned about pregnancy, it seemed, arose from an ardent desire
for its opposite.

There was always a story of a bad mistake. Overtaken by nos-
talgia, or lust, or pity, or gin, or him. The one thing in these days
of AIDS was that there was a way, if you could summon the
courage and sense to do it, of interrupting the story. *The male
pursues the female for the purpose of sexual union.* Now you could
add a footnote to Freud, a fly in the ointment.

Do you have some protection?

You can ask this, these days. You are supposed to ask.

❖ ❖ ❖

Every epoch has its apparatus. Meg recalled with fondness her
early twenties, the Age of the Sponge. You ran it under water and
palpated it until a pristine white foam rose, then worked it up
the canal of yourself. Individually wrapped like an airplane
snack, it came equipped with a cloth strap, so you could tug it
out of yourself in the aftermath, after the afterglow. When you re-
trieved it, a quarter or third of a day later, it slid out of you sog-
gily, blotched with intimate paint, modern art in miniature.

But that was when everything went according to plan. Pregnancy tests came from mistakes. And mistakes came from passion, or passion and booze, or just booze. Once, after drinking
several glasses of an unidentified red drink that resembled
Hawaiian Punch and spouted out of a rubber chicken into a
bathtub at a fraternity party, Meg had accepted an invitation from
one of the brothers to go back to his dorm room and see his fish.
"Japanese fighting fish," he said, as she greeted them woozily,
watching a whirl of gills and bright colors as she tapped at the
glass tank, talking to the fish as if they were dogs: "Here, Lucy.
Here, Ricky." She had turned to find the fraternity brother
stripped of his toga and heading for hers.

The pregnancy test had come up negative. But a week later she'd found tiny crabs beached on the shores of her. She would have preferred, she later told the Catholic Boyfriend, the Japanese fighting fish.

"That's not funny," he said. "That's terrible. You should have reported him to the Authorities."

The Boyfriend, no matter who he was, always had faith in the power of the Authorities.

"It was *grain alcohol* punch," she said. "I was wearing a *toga*. I was in his *dorm room*."

The Boyfriend got mad at her then. "You don't have to *emphasize* everything. You don't have to speak to me as if *English* is my second *language*."

Through trial and error she had learned that date rape, cramps, tampons, affirmative action, and sexual harassment were five topics that failed to endear her to the Boyfriend, no matter who the Boyfriend was. The College Boyfriend didn't even like to hear the word tampon. Both of these, words and tampons, got saved for the Best Friend. In the faux boudoirs of lingerie stores they scrutinized foundation garments, doubted the Wonder Bras, maneuvered around the Mothers and Babies. The Babies might be wailing and sneezing snot, tucked under the Mothers' arms, strollers hung with pastel shoulder bags in front of them. Out of the bags jutted baby bottles sloshing with formula or juice, extra diapers, arrowroot teething biscuits, dolls and games and toys and hats. Meg could not imagine herself hauling around so much gear. It was hard enough for her to keep track of her contact lens rewetting solution.

Two towheaded twins drooling and prattling in their double stroller always seemed to be passing by.

"Ba ba ba," went the Twins.

"Ba ba ba," went the Mother.

"Ba ba ba," went the Twins.

"That's the sort of conversation we'd be having if we had babies," said the Best Friend.

People were always assuming that if you didn't want to have children, it was because you didn't like them. In fact Meg loved children. Children loved Meg. But she loved children the way she loved rain. Rain was great, but you didn't want it raining in your house. For a while now she had been the one nonmother at the Children's birthday party. Inevitably, the Children surrounded her, clambering over her as if she were a jungle gym. In her lap they ran their sticky fingers through her hair, smooched her hands, smeared chocolate on her jeans, wept piteously when their mothers announced it was time to leave.

"You'd be such a good mother. It's obvious," the Mothers said. They wanted to reupholster her life. They would restore her, like a turn-of-the-century Shaker chair. If they found her tumbling down the grassy slope in the backyard with their five-year-olds, green stains on the knees of her stockings, they smiled knowingly at her. And back inside, while she gulped her white wine and picked the white skin off the Brie, they offered up prophecies.

"You'd be so much happier."

"You'd feel fulfilled. When I had Kendra that's how I felt."

"You'd be living for someone else. You'd have a purpose."

Meg didn't know if a purpose was really what she wanted. Not a purpose that needed its diapers changed. Happier, okay. Maybe fulfilled, though the question Meg always had was, what came after fulfilled? More fulfilled? Fulfillered? Did you just spend the next forty years of your life feeling your fulfillment?

Once, when she had slept, unwisely, with her professor of abnormal psychology, she had called her gynecologist back home and said she was worried she might be pregnant. "Do you feel pregnant?" the doctor asked. *Feel* pregnant? Did pregnancy feel more like feeling ill or feeling guilty? Did you feel it in your duodenum or your conscience? Was it possible to know how something felt if you had never felt it before? Meg was suspicious of anyone who wagged the nature card in front of her, people who claimed maternal instinct meant you somehow knew how to care for a baby as soon as it came sliding out of you with its horrific clump of placenta and yelling and blood. She certainly hadn't known beforehand how it would feel to get her period at thirteen for the first time: all of a sudden she had just been dry-heaving in the girls' bathroom when she was supposed to be in industrial arts making a lamp. Title IX had just been instituted at her junior high school, requiring that girls learn to use wood lathes, not just flip crepes in the orange kitchens of the home economics room. That didn't mean the industrial arts teacher, Mr. Fleckston, was sympathetic to her dashing to the bathroom when she was supposed to be shellacking a lamp. No time for shellacking; she had, as the educational booklets proclaimed triumphantly, "reached menarche." Menarche, a place in ancient Greece, a landscape pastel with coliseums in girl-colors.

She liked to imagine her body the way her art history teacher in college had told her people had a few centuries earlier. She would have a classical body, smooth and objectified and, most important, absent of troublesome orifices. She would be all sealed up, nothing gaping or porous. It was a nice fantasy. All her nice fantasies seemed to be about alternate visions of her body. When she fantasized about making love with the Boyfriend, she pictured her face (she liked her face all right, though her teeth could use a little bleaching; that was it: she needed bleached teeth) on a body that was slimmer, taller, bonier. The Fantasy Meg had nicer clavicles. The Fantasy Meg didn't have pregnancy scares.

She knew she was supposed to develop a relationship with the organs clustered below her waist, the uteruses and the cervixes, odd words in an underground vocabulary people rarely used. Our prefixes, her mother liked to say, our suffixes. Meg had grown up during the seventies, when daughters of mothers who had gone through consciousness raising received copies of *Our Bodies, Ourselves* for their thirteenth birthdays. For her thirteenth her mother had given her a copy of her own and a pair of argyle socks. The socks she had worn a lot. The book was full of

enthusiastic inducements to get to know parts of herself she preferred to think of as suburban neighbors. You stood in your garden and waved to them across the street and they waved back,
and at the holidays you complimented them on their lawn decorations. No need to befriend. Befriending your uterus was like
befriending your congressman. You disagreed with his aims, but
you tried to keep things civil. Perhaps you could keep the relationship strictly impersonal, since you objected to the whole
business of reproducing, your uterus's raison d'être. She had an
aesthete's distrust of reproduction.

At the Rite Aid register, she reached for a Skor and a Baby
Ruth from the candy rack. Cravings already, the voice of popular
wisdom whispered. Soon it would be pickles and ice cream, an-
chovies and mince pie. She had never eaten a Skor or a Baby
Ruth, but felt immediately the dark force of woman's intuition
working away at her as she plunked them on the counter beside
the pregnancy test: first he "Skored"; nine months later there was
Baby Ruth. One might learn to communicate entirely in the sym-
bolic and universal language of product names. Here in the late
twentieth century you might not have fidelity to your Significant
Other, but there was always brand loyalty. You had to hand it to
the advertisers for generating that kind of fidelity, in this world of
betrayal and adultery and shifting alliances. She had never dated
a man for more than three years, but she had been using the
same brand of toothpaste since she was nine.

With her purchases in her plastic bag, she sallied forth into
rush hour. She pictured herself a turkey with its bag of giblets, a
bottle of vitamins with the desiccant preservative packet marked
DO NOT EAT lolling at the bottom. As a child she'd loved the
gerbils her mother had gotten for her, the way they ran on their
little wheel in their Habi-Trail, happy prisoners with their water
and food pellets and wood shavings. Then the female had given
birth to six babies and eaten some of them, setting off in Meg a
series of nightmares in which her own mother merrily chewed
off Meg's limbs.

The Boyfriend wasn't due home for another two hours. She tried to walk to Grand Central Station at the careful pace she deemed appropriate for pregnant women. Then, on the subway platform, she thought better of it and pushed in and clutched her strap along with the other passengers. No one else looked the least bit pregnant. Yet all these people had made their first home inside a woman, even the cross-eyed man selling neon light-up yo-yos. She could hardly stand the thought of giving birth to someone who would grow up to be cross-eyed and selling neon light-up yo-yos on the train to Flushing. She directed this thought to what might or might not at that moment be a cluster of cells dividing inside her. *You wouldn't want to be cross-eyed,* she thought. *You wouldn't want to be selling neon light-up yo-yos on the train to Flushing.*

Back at the apartment, she unloaded her purchases on the kitchen table. The two candy bars, the pregnancy test, and a hair-lightening kit for mousy blondes. The hair-lightening kit had been an impulse buy, a desire for an experiment on herself with results that could be controlled. She peeled the gloves off the sheet, which was printed with a long list of instructions it was necessary to read carefully before you started mixing things to-gether. Or else. Or else you might stain your clothes. Or else you might turn your hair a shade of green.

She put the plastic cap on her head and pulled selected strands of hair through it. She painted the strands with a concoc-tion made by mixing one foul-smelling liquid with another foul-smelling liquid. Probably if Meg was pregnant, and if she wanted after nine months to produce a baby that had all its digits working properly, hair-lightening kits would be off-limits. But she didn't want a baby, working digits or not. She wanted gold highlights. She wanted a vodka Collins.

By contrast, the contents of the Clearblue Easy Early Preg-nancy Test were a model of simplicity, nothing more than a foil packet about the size of the wet towelette they gave you in seafood restaurants if you had the lobster with drawn butter.

They had gotten rid of the test tubes and pipettes she remembered from her twenties; they had even gotten rid of the square-shaped plastic cup in which you had been instructed to pee. You always ended up peeing on your hand. Was a square box supposed to be more effective for urine gathering than a round one? It seemed the cup idea in general had not gone over well, as now there was merely a test stick that looked like an elaborate tongue depressor. You were just supposed to pee right on it. However, there were warnings. DO NOT URINATE ON THE WINDOWS. En español: NO ORINE EN LAS VENTANILLAS.

She read the questions and answers provided on the package insert. They weren't the questions she would have asked. She would have asked the existential questions, the why and the what if and the what next. The pamphlet wasn't so interested in existential questions.

Q. What if urine accidentally splashes onto the windows?
A. There is a clear splashguard shield protecting the test area to minimize the effect of accidental urine splash. A colored line in the Reference Window indicates that the test was performed correctly.

Accidental urine splash. A congenital condition, a rock group, a code for nuclear catastrophe. It was difficult to see any link between accidental urine splashes and reference windows and infants in pink flannel blankets.

It was time to remove the test stick from its protective foil pouch and discard the desiccant packet contained therein. It was time to pee. It was time to pee on cue. P on Q. In college she had not done especially well in logic. How did any result follow necessarily from any premise? In her own life, this had never been adequately demonstrated. Virtue never got rewarded. Prudence didn't get you anywhere. The Rich were mean and still looked great.

After five arid minutes on the toilet she got up and called the Best Friend.

"I think I'm pregnant."

"But you're a Planned Parenthood volunteer," the Best Friend said. "Don't they hand out freebie condoms?"

"We were preoccupied with changing the Brita water filter that night."

"Oh, Meg," the Best Friend said. "Do you *feel* pregnant?"

The package insert instructed her to wait three minutes after peeing on the test stick before reading the result. She set an egg timer, grimy with kitchen grease, then placed the test stick on a paper towel and sat down to watch it. She and the Boyfriend had ceremonially given up their TV to a domestic violence shelter a year ago; since then, she'd gotten out of practice at being a viewing audience. But here, at this moment, with hair strands pulled through a pocked plastic cap on her head and peroxide and egg timer and test strip and pee, she might be a performance artist. Soon the test stick would change. Soon the test stick would change and she would perform. She would not be able to help it. She would leap up and exert herself in the service of one of two emotions. Though it would make a less dramatic performance, she was rooting, as a mother at her child's soccer game would in another story, for joy.

Rash

The lettuce, Darren says, must be crisped before he takes it out on the floor for stacking. He places each head in hot water for less than a minute then plunges it into cold water. Afterward he holds the head tenderly against his hip and trims back the filth. This he calls butting. It is a kind of baptism.

When he calls from work, I am very often still in bed. "I butted seven racks of romaine," he'll say. He has a leather holster filled with specialized knives, for taking the rot off produce. We now live in a state with suburbs named Bountiful and Jordan. Down the road from our apartment rises the frosting-white spire of the Mormon temple. Across the street is the Mormon Handicraft Store, rife with quilts.

❖ ❖ ❖

My neighbors believe in celestial marriage, spirit babies, the imminence of the apocalypse, undergarments. In spite of their profligate reproducing, they do not worry about the population problem. They wallow in an excess of certitude. "We have enough canned goods for you, too," one told me. Thus, in the event of nuclear holocaust, I am to have my creamed corn along with the righteous. There is for me a kind of happiness in this. In the company of Mormons, nothing seems tensile or baroque. On the contrary, everything is more or less pureed.

❖ ❖ ❖

In the evenings, Darren is training to be a sales and reservations agent with the airlines. A chubby androgynous security guard waves our car through the gate at dusk. I am not allowed in the building. When I return at midnight, I can often detect a rotting-egg smell off the lake, which hovers glassily beside Route 80. I walked the edges when we first moved here, my ankles plagued by tiny black flies. A tourist office housed in a trailer nearby contained glossy pamphlets, one pimpled and uninformed adolescent at the counter, and a fishbowl teeming with brine shrimp.

❖ ❖ ❖

Ask me why we are here. It is a question worth asking of unhappy people. I work for public radio and am always on the move. Fortunately, the polygamy and skiing in this locale allow for juxtaposition. P. T. Barnum once met Brigham Young and wanted to use him in the show, for instance. Or this: on my first assignment I interviewed a woman who introduced herself as "Mormon Beauty." You may say, did I miss a beat? I did. Now I say, Is that one word or two? Many of our neighbors wear rings engraved with the letters CTR, for Choose the Right. Apparently such reminders are necessary, even for the devout.

❖ ❖ ❖

On Thursday afternoons it is not unusual to see five brides tricked out in identical satin and bustles spilling out of a gated door, the escaped bacterium of Mormon womanhood. Last week I found a small copy of the Book of Mormon on my desk: the portable Mormon. Several passages had been highlighted in yellow. I have my suspicions. "We lie on top of each other with our clothes on," one student intern at the radio station told me. She was wearing a hand-knit sweater with a pink yoke. "We're not even supposed to do that," she said.

I offered her some candy hearts from a bowl on my desk. There are, I have discovered, occasions that demand the ironies of sugared chalk.

◈ ◈ ◈

My mother has crossed over. It certainly did take me a long time to figure it out. This is how: at one of my mother's presidential election parties, a woman told a story about a trip to Fire Island when she saw two men tongue-kissing. The woman sitting next to my mother put on a Richard Nixon mask and we went out to Pancho Villa for margaritas. The bartender said he would give her free margaritas as long as she kept the mask on, but the only way she could drink them was through a straw. Eventually she put her head on my mother's arm, though I couldn't see through Nixon's sockets whether or not her eyes were closed.

◈ ◈ ◈

A London art gallery opened a show recently that featured a painting of Princess Diana spattered with white fluid. Darren gets this information far afield, from the British papers. "In a work called 'Monarch at Bay,' the Queen is shown surrounded by brown paint representing excreta. The artist's strongest 'statement' is 'Black Crown,' a large plastic crown filled with papier-mâché faeces which have been tipped out onto the gallery floor." This is the sort of information that is worth six dollars to me these days.

◈ ◈ ◈

When Darren is not at work, he spends an inordinate amount of time reading the British papers on the toilet, where he sits with a cup of tea. He is sporting a rash along his spinal cord that appeared not long after he moved out here. To myself I call the rash Mary, after his ex-wife. Also after the Virgin, who is known to appear in unexpected places.

❖ ❖ ❖

Mizuna is a small, loose head of jagged, spear-shaped dark green leaves. It has a mild, mustardlike taste. Radicchio, however, is best mixed with other greens, as its bitter taste can be overwhelming. Still, Darren says, most people will be iceberg eaters, despite the watery taste and nutritional value similar to that of cardboard. This is what I've learned from Darren since he started working in a produce department. From me he has learned the meanings of "harbinger" and "euphemism."

❖ ❖ ❖

Darren has one child by his first marriage. That's it, I've told him. We do not often use birth control, as it makes us itch. Because we have been going like this without an accident for four years, Darren is convinced I am infertile. I disagree. On the days I am fertile we keep off each other. Once I was late and I took ginger pills and very large doses of vitamin C. My success has convinced me of the merits of self-supervision.

On Sundays we talk to Darren's daughter on the phone. "You can just come back and be on the radio in New York. There are lots of radios here," she says. Last Sunday it was money she asked for. What did a seven year old need with money, I wanted to know.

"Mom told me to ask."

In the background Mary said, "No, I didn't."

"Yes, you did."

Mary has begun to show up on Darren's chest. In the mornings I examine and kiss it. I am watering all our plants with Miracle-Gro now, which turns water electric blue and makes our plants climb the walls.

❖ ❖ ❖

It is not unnatural to fear that some detail about my family life might slip out. It is a fear I court with trepidation, as I am a public figure of sorts. The Utah board of education has voted to ban all high school clubs rather than allow a gay and lesbian alliance club to meet on campus grounds. My neighbors, the ones who talk about it at all, believe that to be gay is to be comically misguided. I suspect this is not the angle taken by the bishops, who agree about misguided but do not find anything comical in it. "The idea of two guys together," one of my neighbors said. "It's so random." At the end of the school year he is headed on a mission to Nebraska.

❖ ❖ ❖

The rate of hepatitis infection is higher in Utah than in any other part of the country. A family picnic in Utah, or a ward picnic, to which all families attending a neighborhood church would be invited, might include upwards of a hundred people. Jell-O molds with bits of fruit suspended in them are a favorite. Hepatitis is passed like handshakes at gatherings like this. I have been looking into it for a segment I want to do, but infectious disease is not the sort of thing people want broadcast in a state with license plates that say "Greatest Snow on Earth."

❖ ❖ ❖

My mother called after the Pride March. Her lover and another woman got into a fight in front of the Gap. Luckily, Dykes on Bikes came by. The lover got waving at friends, who honked back, an infusion of goodwill. There were some great little madras numbers on sale at the Gap, my mother said. She would send me the money for one.

"You don't have the money to be buying me madras dresses."

"I want to. You'll be able to wear it out."

"Don't worry about it. We don't get out much."

"You should get out. You're young."

"I'm not so young."

"You're not so old you shouldn't be going out. I get out. I'm fifty years old and I get out."

The following Sunday I took Darren out to breakfast at a diner where our waitress is a tippler. He has seen eyes like that back in Ireland, where he grew up. Over coffee I told him about Dykes on Bikes. Next to us some overdressed Mormons were ordering brains.

"She wants me to pay for her au pair," Darren said.

Our waitress came over to take our order.

"What's a large white biscuit?" I asked.

"It's big and it's white and it's bread."

"Is brains and eggs what it sounds like?" Darren asked.

Our waitress likes him. He ordered that. On the pie case an engraved sign said, "Please and Thank You are Magic Words."

We doodled while we waited for our food. The place mats are always the same rough paper printed with small photos of the presidents of the United States in chronological order.

"Your divorce agreement says child care, not au pair," I said.

Darren pointed out that Carter, Reagan, Bush, and Clinton were the only ones of the whole lot who were smiling.

"The law says she can't withhold visitation rights."

Our table was equipped with a little jukebox that played Patsy Cline and Nancy Sinatra at three volumes. Darren pressed the buttons and told me a long joke about Mormons in heaven. Later, when I tried to remember it for telling, all I could recall was the punch line: "They think they're the only ones up here."

❖ ❖ ❖

One joke that is now becoming old is that we will convert. The temple is, after all, within walking distance. It would be wrong, though, to deny that I've been sniffing around for divine intervention. Mary has forbidden us to see Darren's daughter until he can come up with money for an au pair. The other Mary is shooting down his thighs in great swatches of red. At bedtime he makes a paste of Egyptian green clay and water, which I apply to his back. In the night it hardens and cracks, and when we wake, our sheets are sandy, a site of drought.

❖ ❖ ❖

I saw a blind man filling a dish of water for his dog at a drinking fountain and I thought, a rash is not so bad. But it is not my rash. For the first time it occurred to me that I like working in radio because it doesn't taunt the blind.

❖ ❖ ❖

Darren's daughter is getting ready for her communion. We are, in spite of other limitations, allowed to talk to her on the phone. I mop the floor while Darren talks to her. "Did you have rehearsal?" he asks. "Did you taste it? What did it taste like?"

"She said it tasted like cardboard," Darren tells me. "She tried to spit it out and Mary caught her."

Once when I was eight I went to Saint Gertrude's for Mass with a friend and followed her up to the front for a wafer. The man giving it out didn't recognize me. When he asked, I told him I was Jewish, and he told me to go find my seat.

❖ ❖ ❖

My Mormon neighbors are pleasant but candied, like yams. I try to chat with them, fishing for stories. I might as well ask them to arm-wrestle me. The missionaries have the most to say, as they have returned from Guam or Alabama steeped in scripture. There is a rumor among Jews here that if you tell the missionaries who come to your door that you are Jewish, they will step back, as if you are giving off a celestial radium.

❖❖❖

I took a tour of Temple Square when I first moved here, heard the shtick about the pioneers and their handcarts, the seagulls who consumed the plague of grasshoppers and saved the day. A pin was dropped for my benefit in the Tabernacle to prove its acoustic superiority. It did indeed make the sound of a hammer hitting a table, which is meant, I suppose, to count as empirical proof of a Mormon god.

Once I went with Darren to a funeral home for a notary public's signature. On the calendar for the twentieth of June were the words *Inter Ashes Blundell*. Religion and death, it seems, are a much more everyday sort of business than one would imagine.

In between Darren's two jobs we like to take walks around our new neighborhood. Every three or four lawns is a sign that says *Orrin Hatch Now More Than Ever.* A woman sitting on a chaise lounge in the middle of her lawn always holds a hose. A plastic sign pushed in next to the hedge says *Chemical Treatment Today.*

❖❖❖

Each dead Mormon bishop is marked with a monument taller than a tree. His wives are scattered around him, their stones flat to the ground, the word MOTHER carved on each of them. I like to hop from one to another. Just before my mother's mother died she thought she was a little baby and couldn't get anything to eat. My mother told me this while we were sitting Shiva. To me there has never been anything comforting about our religion.

❖❖❖

My mother comes for a visit. She buys mizuna and radicchio for a salad that we eat on the porch steps. By law you can't buy chilled spirits in Utah unless it's beer, so we drink the champagne warm, all of it.

Darren comes home from work with a cardboard box full of fruit lolling inside wrinkled skin, potatoes that have sprouted sturdy shoots, avocados that give under their black knobbled jackets when pushed. I make a guacamole that he eats with chips and his hands.

My mother gives me the madras dress she made such a fuss about on the phone. I like madras. It's encoded with aristocracy and irony. To see a golfer tee off in madras shorts is a comment on the game itself, with its ludicrously small pocked ball and its colonial hold on what little arable land is left. I go indoors and take off my drop-waist dress and put the madras on.

"You look smashing," my mother says.

Darren looks up from his guacamole. "You look smashed."

❖ ❖ ❖

Darren wakes up in the night itching. I go in the kitchen and bend a spear off our aloe plant, which I open and smear across his back.

"I'm hungry," he says. I bring him the rest of the guacamole and some bread, which he wipes in the bowl and eats lying on his belly in bed. His eating is devoted as a child's.

"We have enough canned goods for you, too," I say.

When he's not wearing his glasses, he has to get very close to things, which is why his chin touches the lip of the bowl. "That's good," he says. He contemplates each chip before he eats it. "Did I tell you Mary is pregnant again? She says her lawyer will be calling me."

"What are we going to do, sell the stove and give her the cash?"

We lie down and try to go to sleep. Against my shoulders there is the scrape of dried clay and chip crumbs. I would like Darren to hold my head against him, but what he has for me is his back. On the pads of my fingers I can feel the rash rising to meet me, a faint and unreadable braille.

Holiday

On her first day in Ireland the big news had been an eighteen-month-old boy crushed by a coal lorry, but the upcoming Gaelic football finals eclipsed it. Still, Patrick and his sister voted to make an appearance at the funeral.

"I'll go along," she told them, possessed by a dread of being left alone in a pub at midday.

She thought they would stop home and change into black, but they went as is, he and his sister in green Emmet Tavern shirts with *Up Meath* written in yellow across the left breast. Always the sister wore a short denim skirt and black stilettos with a thick strap at the ankle.

Cars lined the road that led to the church. Outside, a crowd in work clothes or housedresses, milling and smoking. "Jaysus, a terrible shame," someone said. "Next week it'll be somebody else's child." All the milling kicked up dust. There had been little rain in recent weeks, a bright parched autumn. It was indeed altogether against character, everyone said. The overwhelming percentage of idle conversation, she discovered, derived from the weather. Expecting rain, she had from a mail order catalogue purchased the most expensive slicker, a pageant in zippers and Gore-Tex that remained folded in her luggage. She had brought no coat and only two sweaters, which she wore layered. No one else seemed to find the climate chilly.

"So you're back, you are," several men said. They called Patrick "Knacker." Everyone remarked on his great good fortune and referred to her as a poor unfortunate. The assumption seemed to be that they were already married. She rubbed her foot in the dust and noticed his sister's feet, toes crowded in open-toed stilettos, skin hard as ceramic at the heels. There were just below her ankles veiny red sunbursts that looked agonizing.

"You've got yourself a Yank, have ye," another of the men said. She jerked her chin up and produced a fond smile. Wrapped in a bandage, his left hand provided a topic. He had the previous week lost most of a finger and part of another to a hacksaw.

"That's awful," she said. There seemed in general to be too much avoidable maiming and killing.

And yet, the man said, he still had eight and a half to go.

The sister had a high, crackling voice and an accent that sounded like a put-on. She swore she would take two Valium before she went up to Dublin for the match. It was her eldest son that played for the Meath team. The quarterfinals and semifinals had rendered her useless, she said, useless. She should, she said, just sell her ticket to the finals, as she would see only bits of the match through her hands. For Patrick's benefit his sister and the man with the missing digits set to reporting the key plays in the semifinal match. The son had played well, had kept his hands clean when a fight broke out. "Jaysus," Patrick kept saying, "Jaysus."

After a time she felt it advisable to say something. Anything. The astonishing resemblance between them, she remarked. "You might be twins."

"Twins!" the sister said, jostling him, then declared the ten years between them made her almost his mum.

He at last introduced her as his fiancée, and in a pub down the road got her a glass of Guinness and black currant. It tasted treacly. She gulped and dripped it on her sweater. "Has Patrick not taught you how to hold your drink?" the sister asked. The twins comment had for some reason put her on the outs.

❖ ❖ ❖

His daughter. His daughter was a great devotee of hers, a fact that might, she saw, up her credibility. As his ex-wife was Irish, Clare looked the part, freckled and milk-skinned, until she opened her mouth.

The sister called her two daughters in from the street. Soon they were clamoring, soon they had their hands in her hair.

"I like this curl," the bigger one said, groping at her forehead. "Will I snip it to keep for my own? Will I?"

They wanted jockey backs. They wanted to take her to Mc-Cormack's for packets of crisps and then to the crumbling castle where a Hollywood movie had been filmed. They wanted to prick her finger at the Jealous Man and Woman, where people left rusty pins for the curing of warts.

"He wanted to be a woman and she wanted to be a man," the younger one said.

I'll get tetanus, she thought but did not say.

She learned what a jockey back meant when the bigger one leapt on her. Nicola, eleven and already the height of an adult, felt light as a cat on her back, lighter by far than Clare. En masse, they walked up the hill to McCormack's. The two daughters began to sing. "C'mon you little boys in green," were the words, over and over. "Little" came out "li-ill." The younger one declared that if Meath won everyone would get the Monday following off, but the boys' school got it off regardless.

"How can that be?" she said.

"That's not fair," she said.

No one deemed it necessary to take this up with her.

Clare caught up to her and took her hand. The adults had gone on ahead, had already entered the pub.

She began to try to put together in her head an idea of Gaelic football. From passengers on the plane she had learned it combined soccer, American football, and basketball. These analogies simply blurred the matter, exhausted her powers of imagination. And yet it was important to show an interest. And yet it was mandatory to show an interest.

"What's it like, Gaelic football?" she asked the girls.

"Oh, it's brilliant, absolutely brilliant!"

This seemed to sum it up.

The publican had a great fondness for American women, though this did not, as she might have thought, translate into conversational engagement. He was, rather, preoccupied with giving advice to the sister as to how to care for her son. He mustn't be coddled, the publican insisted. And yet you'd want to give the boy a nice joint of meat the day before the match, nicer than you might ordinarily purchase.

"Will ye have a word with Junior, then, for a price reduction on the T-bones?" the sister crowed.

She inferred, of course, that the butcher's name was Junior. Still, she would have liked to be brought up to speed. To be let in on things. Nonetheless, a great many pints were poured for her, so that she got tipsy and full on Guinness in the middle of the afternoon and had to fight off a continuous urge to belch. A lack of other patrons meant the children could run wild without fear of scolding. She found them climbing on the windowsills in the women's bathroom.

"Enough, enough," she said. She secured for them more packets of crisps and several pound coins for the jukebox in the rear lounge. Clare, in velvet overalls and matching hat, wailed when the sisters vetoed her selection.

"You hear enough of those songs at home," she said.

"No I don't! I don't ever!"

A good deal of flailing of arms and legs began on the part of the two sisters.

"See how fun it is?" she gasped, boogying sweatily in her Aran knit.

Clare was persuaded to join them and soon afterwards knocked the pint of Guinness off the table.

"Now you've done it," the little one said.

"Eejit." She gave Clare a reproving look as she knelt for the shards. Already she had adopted this locution.

"You hate me," Clare said, and ran off to her father.

❖❖❖

At the weekend they attended a hurling match, not Mass. An alarming clacking of sticks predominated, so close to heads that she became convinced someone would suffer a brain injury. "Is this like Gaelic football?" she asked, shielding her eyes. For this question and her squeamishness she was ribbed and dismissed.

The children got up a game of tag in the long grass beyond the sidelines. "You're it, you're it," they shouted at her, the sisters, and Clare and four or five children she had never laid eyes on. Thin and fast, they made her feel as if she and Clare were overfed. Earlier in the day she'd bought a roll of fruit-flavored toffees and distributed them. It had been as if she were dispensing gold coins among serfs, except for Clare, who had whined for a bottle of Lilt. "You just had a bottle of Lilt," she'd pointed out, a statement which did nothing to quell further demands for bottles of Lilt.

Breathless, she could only catch Clare, who set to yelling, "Not fair, not fair."

"In what way is it not fair?" she asked.

Clare slapped her hip and dashed away from her.

His daughter was, after all, like his ex-wife, all unpleasantness beneath the cream-and-sugar exterior. Once on Christmas morning they had stopped by to bring Clare her gifts, and Fiona had cornered her on her way to the bathroom. "Can I get a mimosa for you?" she'd asked. Then, just as casually: "Did he get drunk and fuck you Christmas Eve? That's always how it was with me."

He had gotten drunk and not fucked her.

Late in the afternoon an ice-cream truck plowed through the tall grass and set up shop, sending all the children begging for money. Clare would not be satisfied by anything less than a Popsicle and a bottle of Lilt.

"Would you like a Popsicle for yourself, love?" Patrick asked.

No, not at all, she said. She felt an alarming and unfamiliar urge for a pint of Guinness.

"Grand, then," he said, kissing her.

Clare demanded a kiss as well. Patrick bestowed it with great ceremony, then licked her Mr. Softy cone. "You ruined it, ruined it!" she cried, a newly acquired habit of repetition.

"I did no such thing."

❖ ❖ ❖

She was unaccountably happy when Clare got stung. By a wasp, on her inner thigh, a round red welt rising. At this Clare commenced to hopping and shrieking near the adults.

"Come let me see," she said. She felt herself smiling as she beckoned.

Patrick's sister came over to inspect and proclaimed the need for vinegar and raw onion, else the poison would travel to her brain and kill her.

"I quite doubt that," she said.

Again she had managed to say the wrong thing entirely.

The walk to the food store took a number of minutes, all silent but for Clare's lamentations. A very overweight shopkeeper in an apron white with floury handprints confirmed that the poison would indeed go to the child's head without the employment of an onion and vinegar. The shopkeeper procured and sliced the onion in half, then rubbed it and a handful of vinegar on the welt.

"There now," she said. On her nose the shopkeeper displayed a wart of fantastic proportions.

There must be some cure for that, she thought cruelly.

Clare paused in her bawling and seemed to judge it unnecessary to continue. "I could've died, you know," she said as they walked back to the hurling match.

"Everybody dies."

"But I could've died today, and then you would've felt bad."

"You'd like for me to feel bad, wouldn't you?"

"No," she said. The hand she offered up was filthy with dirt and vinegar. "You'll give me a jockey back, won't you?"

"But it'll scrape your sting."

"No it won't."

In this manner it was settled. She hoisted Clare on her back, and they went to find Patrick, who must be shown the doctored welt.

"Who's winning?" she asked when they found him. It was clear that she had not even bothered to figure out which team was which.

"We are," he said, then knelt and gathered Clare to him. "My poor pussycat, my Toffo girl," he said.

It struck her that he was not so much a bad father (as his ex-wife charged) as someone following a poorly written script for fatherhood. In his actions he appeared stiff and wooden, more like a stepfather. At home in New York Clare did have a stepfather, that and two new half-brothers. It had been deemed by Fiona necessary for Clare to refer to her stepfather as Daddy, so as not to confuse the two boys. This often resulted in Clare relating a story of activities she had done or things she had seen with her daddy. When corrected, she would only laugh and say, "Not this daddy, the other daddy."

It ripped him up inside, this business of the other daddy.

"My brave girl," he was saying. "A Popsicle? A can of Lilt?"

"Lilt," Clare said. The novelty of Irish soda still hadn't worn off.

"Another Lilt?" she said. "You'll have a tummy ache."

He threw her a look that discouraged further interference.

Once Clare had visited them for a three-week stretch in the summer that culminated in a disagreement in a toy store. They had gone in for computer Scrabble, to give the two of them respite from Scrabble marathons. Yet a computerized Wheel of Fortune had reduced her to begging. Patrick had bought it for her.

She herself had walked on ahead, the heels of her sandals catching in the soft hot blacktop in the parking lot.

In the car they'd fought. She'd uttered the words *fuck* and *fucking,* had made Clare cry, had been ordered to pull the car to the side of the road so that he and his daughter could hail a cab and be driven home by a sane person.

And yet when it came down to it, she'd been a more than adequate surrogate. She had invented a game whereby she and Clare filled two coolers with water and placed them in strategic locations outside their apartment building, ambushed each other in their bathing suits with cupfuls. Whole afternoons had been spent in video arcades, driving video racing cars at breakneck speeds through computer-generated Londons and Parises.

They returned with bottles of Lilt for everyone, her included.

"Try it, it's good," Clare said.

"I know what it tastes like. It's just like the sodas back home."

"No, it's not."

"I don't want it," she said. "Go give it to one of the girls."

"Okay," Clare said, and skipped off, grudgeless.

She heard her name called, the new cadences of it in the mouths of Irish girls, and went to join the tag game.

"Leave it to them," Patrick said. "You're not a child."

❖ ❖ ❖

Clare and her cousins had been out in the street playing ball and trading riddles. Children of a certain age seemed to take inordinate pleasure in brainteasers. They came in and accosted her on the couch, their cheeks and limbs cold against her. "Now see if you can get this one," Clare said, proceeding even after she insisted she wasn't in the mood for riddles.

It involved holding up a hand, fingers spread, and marking

off each finger with a Johnny. "Johnny, Johnny, Johnny, Johnny, whoops, Johnny, whoops, Johnny, Johnny, Johnny, Johnny," Clare said. "Whoops" marked the downward slope from index finger to thumb and back. "Now you do it. Do exactly as I did."

She obeyed, nine Johnnys and two whoopses.

"No, no! She's wrong, she's wrong!" Delighted squeals from all quarters. She was pressed upon to observe the activity again and then to perform again herself, after which she was declared once and for all a dunce.

"I'm not playing anymore," she said.

"She hates losing at Scrabble, too," Clare told them. "Once she pushed the board off the table."

This was indeed true; Clare had been smug one time when she'd used up all her letters in one turn with the word *boarder*.

She mutely beseeched Clare not to bring up the incident in the toy store. It would make her seem monstrous, unreasonable. Already she could feel the sympathies shifting from her to Clare, her hold on the two girls loosening. Did they want a jockey back? Did they want to play with her hair? No, not until she figured out the riddle.

"I have no idea," she said. "It's a stupid riddle."

"Look," Clare said, then went through the nine interminable Johnny's and two whoopses again and crossed her arms over her chest with great emphasis. "You didn't cross your arms!"

"But you always cross your arms like that," she pointed out. It was Clare's modus operandi, her raison d'être.

"Too bad, you lose," Clare said.

The girls ran off to a bedroom, leaving her alone in the living room with a carton of milk she realized was curdled. Cartons of milk could be found in various locations throughout the house. Like lanterns, she thought, recalling her mother's fondness for candles. A wave of homesickness she had not anticipated hit and drenched her. Perhaps a phone call to the States could be arranged. But not now, not on the sister's bill. All of the furniture in the room was threadbare and unraveling. And yet the display case wedged into the corner held the most stunning specimens of Waterford crystal, plate and bowl and decanter. She tried the door to the case and found it locked. Up close she could see a fine thin dust settled on all the crystal. It struck her that every house she had visited had not only the same layout but contained roughly the same objects. A crucifix. Cheap reproductions of saints on the walls, particularly in bathrooms. A requisite amount of unused Waterford crystal displayed in this manner. Photos of the children in communion clothes—boys in suits, girls in white organza like little brides. She recalled Patrick's story of his mother knitting him a communion suit, all wool. But it had been scratchy, had caused him to break out in a rash. He had insisted on a store-bought ensemble—had not, he said, wanted to be the odd one out.

In the kitchen they were all smoking up a storm, too much for her to join them. The brother-in-law left for a while, then returned with an armful of Carlsberg in the can. For her, two cans of Bulmer's hard cider, for which she had earlier expressed a liking. These he tossed to her from the foyer.

"How are ye, darlin'?" he asked. He was nice. He had an ulcer.

"Not a bother," she said, another borrowed locution. She was aware that this sounded fake.

A British game show requiring an expertise in cooking was playing on the television. A disagreement over sultanas arose, and then another over braising. From the context she ascertained that sultanas were some form of raisin.

"My God," she said to herself, "my God." She realized she had not eaten since a slice of brown bread that morning.

❖ ❖ ❖

A yeast infection heralded the beginning of the second week. She had not thought to bring her usual remedies: tea tree and lavender oils, acidophilus, garlic pills. Patrick and Clare were instructed to buy plain yogurt and a bulb of garlic from Super Quinn while she lay in the Gaelic football player's bed and scratched at herself. The athlete had not yet made an appearance, as he was training at some undisclosed site. In a team photograph she found in a desk drawer, she studied him: the sister's and brother-in-law's former good looks, not yet ruined by cigarettes and drink. That she could see. A minnow of desire ran through her, for someone wholesome. For someone not dissolute and infected. The itching was unholy, worse than any she'd ever suffered. She considered asking the sister for a remedy but could not overcome her embarrassment, could not form the words.

"It's all the Guinness and cider," Patrick volunteered as he handed her the plastic shopping bag and dragged Clare out of the room.

She applied the yogurt to her labia, then peeled a garlic clove and inserted it into her vagina. The sting blotted the itching.

❖ ❖ ❖

A ceremonial visit to an elderly great-aunt, who suffered from innumerable ailments and a dowager's hump, was unavoidable.

She had never heard of a dowager's hump.

"Come here." The sister pushed simultaneously at the back of her head and her stomach, until she was doubled up. "Like that," she said, "with a great hump like a camel's out your back."

Clare insisted she had no memory of the aunt and would not go.

"She sent you a twenty-pound note for your communion. Don't be cheeky," Patrick warned.

The aunt was small and myopic and smelled like scented toilet tissue. It would not have been accurate to say she was unfriendly, although for the first time since they had been calling on his relatives, they were not pressed upon to drink successive cups of weak tea. In fact no tea was offered. Nor was it possible for Clare to obtain a bottle of Lilt.

The aunt's house was a replica of the sister's minus the milk cartons. A path had been worn in the carpet between the aunt's chair and the television, as she had edema and shuffled. She sighed a good deal and fussed with the hem of her skirt, her feet propped up on an ottoman. Her feet were fantastic, terrible, the ankles swollen to the size of kneecaps.

"I'm bored," Clare kept saying.

Patrick fabricated a number of questions about the aunt's medications, in response to which the aunt explained in great detail her schedule for taking liver tablets and stomach tablets and blood pressure tablets.

"At times I am very poorly," she said, shaking her head, martyred, then asked about Fiona. Patrick reported that she was grand and had cut her hair.

"Now that's a pity, with that lovely red hair," the aunt said.

There was a protracted silence, in which she and Patrick shifted in their seats. The aunt squinted at some point just above her head. She had yanked her own hair into a ponytail to disguise how dirty it had gotten. There was no shower in the sister's house, only a bath with a handheld showerhead that produced a forlorn and tepid trickle. At first she had bathed every day, but she had discerned that Patrick's relatives found this habit indulgent. Yogurt seemed to be leaking through her jeans. It occurred to her that on the chair, upholstered in faded violet fabric with scratchy veins of gold threaded through it, she might leave a stain.

❖ ❖ ❖

"What's a knacker?" she asked him. They were on their way to Dublin for the match, him and his sister and the brother-in-law smoking with the windows closed. She used the word *miasma*.

Everyone laughed. People in other cars were hanging dangerously far out their windows with the purpose of waving yellow-and-green or red-and-green flags. "Mayo cunts," the brother-in-law said, cutting off a car all done out in green and red streamers. "A knacker is a tinker," he said. "A traveler."

"Tinker, traveler, tinker, traveler," Clare sang.

"Knock it off," said Patrick.

The three of them were playing a game of Old Maid in the backseat, Clare between them.

"You're not paying attention," Clare said.

She saw that she again held the Old Maid, a fat caricature in an apron with a kerchief tied on her head. She had played six games with Clare that morning and each time had found herself in possession of the Old Maid.

She scrutinized the back of the card. "You've marked it, to make sure you never get it."

"Don't be silly," Clare said.

"I'm out," she said, slapping all the cards face down.

Clare grabbed at them. "All pairs?"

"Close enough."

They were careening along a road dotted at regular intervals with pubs. Outside them children with flags waved and cheered. The brother-in-law proposed they stop in for a quick one. Then, down the road, another. She and Clare ate several packets of vinegary crisps while the others drained pints at the Haggard Inn and then at a pub that smelled alternately of mothballs and soot.

No, Patrick explained, she could not manage it the rest of the way to Dublin, as she had never learned how to drive a stick shift. The brother-in-law and the sister found this preposterous.

"But true nonetheless," said Patrick, giddy with lager.

Beside a trailer painted purple, purple laundry flapped on a line, and a black dog reared into the road and almost got hit.

"Those are tinkers," the brother-in-law said, then broke out singing. "Oh the travelers gone settlin' and the settlers gone travelin'."

Clare was holding up the Old Maid, culled from the cards she'd thrown down.

"But you can't mark cards," she snapped.

"You realize," Patrick whispered in her ear, "you're being a pain in the ass."

The cards were pressed into her lap. She hated the cards. Eight hundred, she thought, would not be an exaggerated estimate of the number of games of cards she and Clare had played. She saw it would please her to announce an intention to end this charade between her and Patrick, this crenellated act of fondness. Surely a year from this moment she would look back as through a telescope and revile her next gesture. And yet. And yet she knew with certainty that she would roll down her window and to the great dismay and censure of all passengers fling into the wind the cards, where they would catch and scatter and eventually, in all the dust, settle.

Vaudeville

We are on our way to visit Vanessa. Squeezed between Melanie and Reesha in the front seat of Melanie's old Valiant, I twist my hands in my lap. "Whose idea was this?" Reesha whispers.

Melanie is laughing. When we stop at a red light, she turns and fixes a smile on us. "We really look like men in these outfits!" she says. "Remind me to get a picture of us."

I might be the only one worried that our gag won't go over. It's possible Vanessa wasn't paying attention to the movie we took her to see at the plush Syosset Triplex, where the curtain rolls up in slow scarlet waves and the screen stretches all the way to the edge of your peripheral vision. She sat on the aisle, her IV standing sentry next to her, me on her other side. Every time I glanced at her, I caught the startling smooth silhouette of her skull. The slow drip of solution into a plastic tube that snaked toward her arm mesmerized me. A bright moment on the screen illuminated two heads in front of us merged in an openmouthed kiss. I pretended I did not notice Vanessa, slack-jawed, not watching the movie at all.

The plot of this movie turned on Julie Andrews disguising herself as a man. I remember her careful straight mannish walk, her somber suits and bow ties, the tingling pleasant shock of her

slender white arms when she appeared in a sleeveless dress toward the end of the movie. A yellow frock. Or maybe this was
the Julie Andrews I knew in *The Sound of Music*? That Julie Andrews, singing in the Alps, kept intruding when I tried to get the
plot of this new movie fixed in my mind. I went along with
Melanie's gimmick for any number of reasons: because she has
always been the ringleader, because I have always been accused
of dragging my heels where so-called fun is concerned, because
cross-dressing vectors us off into distraction. Some people, it is
said, will do anything for a distraction.

❖ ❖ ❖

Vanessa is at home with her family again, in their new house in
Locust Valley. The sod for the lawn has not even been laid yet, so
her house sprawls in dusty dirt, one of only ten in Oak Neck Es-
tates. All of us—me, Melanie, Reesha—live in the next town
over. We live in flimsy split ranches and winterized bungalows
packed in tight rows along the beach, built that way so every
owner could boast a water view. All of us pretend not to be in-
timidated by Vanessa's broad, blacktopped driveway as we pause
for Melanie to snap a photo of us in front of the wrought-iron
gate. She slings one arm around a statuette of a black coachman
carrying a lantern. As I walk by, I rap the statuette's red-and-
white-striped cap with the heel of my hand. I hate tacky lawn
decorations. I hate the pair of black lanterns with electric lights
burning in them even though it's the middle of the day.

As we approach the front door, Melanie pulls ahead of us.
She might be hurrying to a surprise party. All our trips to Vanessa
this past year—first to the local hospital, then to the colossal cancer hospital on the Upper East Side—have been marked by
Melanie's irrepressible good cheer. I could object to this, but on
what grounds? Who am I to say how you're supposed to conduct
yourself in the presence of a seventeen year old who has been in
the hospital for a year? The rest of us have gone to the hospital

for sprained ankles, childhood fevers, tonsillectomies. Melanie once had an operation for the removal of corns from her feet. This is the sum total of it. A year in the hospital, and when you get out, your whole wardrobe is out of style.

Vanessa has a stepmother who dislikes me. The first time we met I was carving my initials and Vanessa's into a birch tree in their front yard. There was Vanessa, squatting next to me in a pink dress and matching ballet flats. We were ten and reading *Harriet the Spy* together. We were jealous—me because Harriet got to hide in dumbwaiters and write in her black-and-white notebook about everyone she knew; Vanessa just because Harriet was allowed to wear overalls and sneakers. I carved KS + AG FRIENDS FOREVER in the birch bark with my pocketknife while Vanessa cursed Eddie Grandinetti and all boys, and we agreed that Eddie Grandinetti was a stupid name; it was like naming your kid Tommy Salami or Lizzy Gowizzy.

"And if you married him your name could be Vanessa Grandinessa!" I told her. Vanessa bent one knee of her white tights in the dusty dirt and reached between her legs. "Stop, Kay," she gasped. "I can't hold it in, I'm gonna pee in my pants." I was laughing too and wiping my runny nose on my shirtsleeve when Angelina shot out the front door and yelled something at us in Italian. Vanessa grabbed my hand and said we had to go inside.

After that invitations to Vanessa's did not come so frequently. Angelina was suspicious of me anyway, suspicious of girls who played sports, girls with mothers who worked outside the home, girls who read too much, people who were reduced to living in beach houses year-round. She encouraged us to play board games like Clue or Life, or to help her make desserts: Jell-O layered with whipped cream in fancy parfait glasses, wobbly green or orange Jell-O molds with tiny slivers of pineapple suspended in them. When she didn't hear noise upstairs, she found reasons to tiptoe up and spy on us. Once she marched in and snatched a copy of *Wuthering Heights* out of my hands and snapped it shut, causing me to lose my place in the book. Vanessa and I had been reading aloud to each other, the two of us pressed together beneath a reading lamp in Vanessa's father's study. "Pretty girls ruin their eyes reading all the time," Angelina said, and made us follow her downstairs, where we were permitted to watch a soap opera called *Edge of Night* and eat Perugina chocolates wrapped in blue-and-silver foil. Apparently Angelina did not worry that chocolates could hurt a pretty girl's figure.

❖ ❖ ❖

I haven't seen Angelina since she found out she was pregnant. Two months ago she gave birth to a fat baby girl. I saw blurry Polaroids of the baby tacked up next to Vanessa's bed in the hospital, but Angelina and I never ran into each other at the hospital. After the baby's birth she became anemic and had to stay in bed. I did run into Vanessa's father pacing the halls of Sloan-Kettering, an unlit cigarette or a stale Danish in his hand. One evening when Vanessa was fast asleep, we slumped on stools outside her room, and he confessed he'd wanted the baby to be a son. He'd planned to name him Walt, after Walt Disney. "Daughters," he said, tilting his head in Vanessa's direction, "are a lot of trouble."

I said I thought Walter would be a hard name for a boy to manage in school.

"Not Walter," he said. "Walt."

"Next time I'll be sure to keep my fingers crossed for a boy," I said, and wished Vanessa would wake up.

❖ ❖ ❖

Angelina opens the door, her wiry black hair yanked up and tied high on her head in a way that looks like she's in a hurry, her eyes dark as brewed coffee and lined underneath as if with gray chalk. A bad cover-up job. She steps back and allows us to crowd the foyer.

"This is obviously some kind of a joke," she says.

Melanie explains that it's from the movie.

"That's very sweet of you," Angelina says. The tone of voice she uses reminds me of my sixteenth birthday, when a dozen roses got delivered to me at home. They were from my parents.

That's very sweet of you.

I take off my hat and hold it at my side. "Just visitors, then. We don't have to do the thing with the outfits."

"But the outfits are the whole thing," Melanie says.

❖ ❖ ❖

This past year I memorized the inside of a cancer hospital and the subways and tunnels up to street level that get me there. I helped Vanessa pick clumps of hair off her pillow and save them in a sealed plastic bag. I held a kidney tray for her while she dry-heaved into it. During this she made sounds that were almost words. It took me a while to stop asking what she was trying to say.

Look, Angelina: we're seventeen. That's something I'd like to have the guts to say. Years ago, when Angelina had just married Vanessa's father, Vanessa and I saw her pressed against him in the living room, unlit except for the flames from two white candles flickering on a low table. We stood against the wall in the hall-way and listened to Angelina purr in Italian, and we saw her shove Vanessa's father against the sofa with a motion in her hips. He ran one hand through his thin silvery hair while she kissed him hard on the mouth. "Paolo, Paolo," she said. I didn't realize that this word was Italian for Paul.

"In the middle of the night I hear her saying that," Vanessa whispered in my ear. Then we went back to Vanessa's bedroom and whispered about Angelina as if she was a scandalous soap opera star we'd seen on the street: Can you believe that dress she wore? That red nail polish on those claws of hers? Whenever I pictured Angelina, she was exhaling smoke, a silver cigarette holder between her bejeweled fingers. It did not make any differ-ence that in real life she wore only a thin gold wedding band, or that she always smoked her Marlboro Lights holderless. "Does she always speak with that accent?" I asked Vanessa. "Or is it an act?"

"Oh no," Vanessa said. "It's no act. Her relatives don't speak a word of English."

Angelina's accent only made her more of a celebrity. More sophisticated, more scandalous. I did not know that she was closer in age to Vanessa and me than she was to Vanessa's father.

When Angelina made us breakfast, she flitted around the kitchen in a satin bathrobe and black summer sandals. We each got half a grapefruit with half a maraschino cherry in the center, and spoons with teeth around the edges to eat them. Then buckwheat pancakes, with a thick blueberry syrup Angelina had made herself from blueberries we'd picked, boiled for hours over low heat with lots of sugar. Vanessa and I knew all this was about sex, but we only communicated our understanding through blushes and innuendo. It was several months of listening to Angelina in the night before Vanessa said to me, "They were doing it. That's why she says his name that way."

After that we did not creep into the hall late at night anymore. We had solved the mystery, so listening seemed voyeuristic, dirty. But we resented Angelina, with her good moods and perfect pancakes and sexy satin robes; and when she slapped frozen waffles in the toaster oven for us or wandered downstairs with a red flannel bathrobe belted loosely at her waist, a Marlboro dangling between two fingers, we watched her with an unspoken glee as she exhaled and sighed and sifted through her unpaid bills. Angelina hadn't been doing it.

❖❖❖

Angelina looks at her watch. "Porca madonna! Where's that nurse?" she says. "Go ahead," she tells us. We climb the stairs, tripping on our trousers.

Vanessa lies on a hospital cot between the window and her canopy bed, covered with fashion magazines. *Mademoiselle,* with a picture of a woman in a plaid skating outfit gathering her bright, coppery hair into a French twist; *Cosmopolitan,* with its woman wearing a V-neck dress that shows perfect, powdered breasts. This month the dress is ice-blue. This month a single sapphire hangs suspended between those breasts.

"Da-da-da!" Melanie sings, shuffling into the room and lifting her straw hat up and down on her head like a vaudeville actor.

Vanessa smiles and lets her gaze fall slowly on each of us.

"Do you get it?" I have to know if she gets it.

"Of course she gets it," Melanie says.

"You guys look great," says Vanessa.

"We brought a hat for you, too." Melanie places a black chauffeur's cap on Vanessa's head. We smile at her and Reesha says, "It looks good," in the same reassuring tone she has always used when she has to give an opinion. Always the moderator, always the mediator, Reesha's response is always noncommittal: *It's fine, it looks good.* Once, when Melanie drew out four strong Irish cigarettes she'd stolen from her grandfather and offered them to us during a winter walk on the beach near my house, Vanessa and I each took one and tried to smoke. While we coughed into our cupped hands and watched Melanie for how to inhale, Reesha walked ahead of us at the water's edge, the ash of her unsmoked cigarette falling in the water. "Thank you for the cigarette," she said to Melanie when the cigarette had burned down to half its length. She dipped it daintily in the water, then wrapped it in a tissue and put it in her coat pocket.

Vanessa doesn't try to remove or adjust the chauffeur's hat. It's a relief for us not to see her bald head—the skin high on her forehead translucent, with a few pale blue veins barely visible beneath; the vulnerable, startling bump just above where her skull joins her spine; the shock of so much brown hair gone. It's been a year, I always tell myself. It shouldn't be such a shock anymore.

Melanie starts to clear the magazines off the bed so we can lie across it and talk. "You know if you want them I have a huge stack of *Cosmos* and *Glamours.* For a while I even went on this celebrity stint and started getting *People*." She is chattering now, but Vanessa doesn't seem to be listening. She is staring out the window at a hat blowing across the yard.

"Do you want me to bring them over?" Melanie asks.

"Someone should get that hat," Vanessa says.

"Oh!" says Reesha. "It's mine! You didn't get to see the whole outfit I put together."

"Maybe go out and get it." Vanessa sighs and settles back on her pillows. I watch some greenish-yellow fluid drip into a plastic bag attached to her bed. In the hospital, someone would have put a towel over that. I think of Vanessa and me at sleep-away camp, Camp Meadowlark in Maine. Her pulling the crotch of her one-piece bathing suit to the side and saying, "Wouldn't it be great to pee like the boys? You could just whip it out, I've seen my cousins do it." And me holding the door to prevent it from swinging open while she was peeing, staring at my sunburned nose in the cloudy bathroom mirror because I was embarrassed to look at Vanessa, embarrassed even by the sound of the stream of pee hitting the toilet water.

Now Vanessa doesn't pee. It drips out of her through a clear plastic tube. This is something I would like to ask her about.

Reesha leaves to get her hat. We listen to her gallop down the stairs, then watch her move into the middle of the yard. She is shapeless in her enormous suit, her straight black hair whipping across her face as she bends for the cap. Just as she reaches for it, a gust of wind sends it against a bush, and we watch her dive for her hat. Melanie is right: high school girls dressed as men in suits *is* a distraction. I don't mind watching Reesha dive for a hat in the yard. What I dread is the idea of Melanie making us act, or sing.

I decide that I need to get out of this room for a minute. Even if it is just a minute, it will be a whole minute without having to see Vanessa's skull and the bag with the green fluid in it. That would be a good minute. I excuse myself, saying I need a glass of water.

I start down the stairs. The house is a split-level, with a giant sitting room wedged between the first and second floors. I hear the sounds of someone playing the piano and a thin voice singing in another language: *Lascia la spina cogli la rosa.* La rosa must be the rose; I don't know about the rest. Angelina's back is to me, but she turns as I make my way down the stairs.

"I was just coming down for some water."

"There's coffee if you want. How is she?"

I never know what to say to this. I'm always falling into the gap between what I want and the way it is.

"She seems better, I think," Angelina says. If I wait, she always fills in the gap for me. "I tell her father I think she is better all the time."

"Yes," I say, "soon things will change." We go downstairs, and Angelina pours me a cup of coffee. All the way up the stairs again, I hold the cup near my nose and smell the cinnamon she has sprinkled on the top.

When I come back into the bedroom, Melanie is telling a long story that I have already heard about fending off a football player from the Oyster Bay team. Oyster Bay is only the next town over, but the way Melanie talks, you would think it's Australia. None of us know anyone from Oyster Bay except this one guy Melanie fended off. I perch on the bed with my hands around my coffee mug. Coffee makes me feel as if I am older than the other people in this room. I might be the one in charge.

"You know," Vanessa says, "Angelina made all this food yesterday—these little almond cookies shaped like moons, and cannolis. You should have some."

At this Melanie is on her feet. "We could get some . . . or we could eat and then come back up . . ."

"Why don't you do that," Vanessa says.

I start to follow Melanie and Reesha, but then I look at Vanessa. She isn't saying anything, but she's telling me to stay.

"I'll be down in a minute," I say.

I sit down next to her.

"Tell me about school," she says.

There are not many things to tell about school. Melanie got a speaking role in the school musical again; Reesha and I got dancing chorus. This means we'll stand in the back row during all the ensemble scenes and gesture broadly with our hands. We will be instructed to move our mouths soundlessly. Vanessa knows about this; she was dancing chorus in *The Music Man* with us in ninth grade. I got the old lady costume, with a hat that looked like a cake iced with big pink roses. She and Reesha, for being short, got little girl costumes, dresses with sailor suit bibs.

"This year we're doing *Once upon a Mattress,*" I tell her.

Vanessa laughs. "You're not just saying that to make me feel better about my bedsores?"

"No."

I gaze out the window at her dog, Amos, straining on his leash, Angelina trying to pull him back onto the front walk. Amos scrabbles around in the dirt, stirring up a cloud of dust.

"Do you have a prom date?" she asks.

I shrug. "I had to ask him. Otherwise I wouldn't have."

"He said yes?" She is leaning forward now, perfectly still except for the blinking of her eyes. I watch the steady drip from her IV.

"He's a junior. That tennis player Neil I told you about. I figured the options were wait for some loser to ask me or ask who I wanted to ask." I don't tell Vanessa that this sentence sums up the major dilemma in my life for the past six months. It's hard to imagine how such logic comes across to a person who's been hooked up to tubes in the hospital for a year. Four seasons. A year.

We both watch Amos resist Angelina, leaping up only to be yanked back.

"If my father saw her treating Amos like that he'd have a fit," Vanessa says. "I think she's got her hands full with me and the baby. She can't handle the dog."

"Yeah," I say. "That must be hard on her."

"Kay," she says, "I want you to know I'm not doing so well."

I set my coffee cup down on top of a stack of magazines.

"I don't really know what that means. I just wanted to tell you."

"Okay," I say.

"I think what it means is I might die."

I look up and see the sliver of Vanessa's body outlined by the sheets. Once she had bigger breasts than I did. Once we went to Macy's together and bought Maidenform bras, an A-cup for me, a B-cup for her. At first we thought I'd be the B and she the A, and ended up trading by passing them under the changing room stall.

"I can't even think about that," I say.

Neither of us says anything for a minute. Vanessa's hand rests on the metal safety bar of her cot. I put my hand over hers. We sit like that until the room whirls white around me and I hear someone call my name. I get up and lean over to kiss her. As I lean close I smell antiseptic and iodine and soap.

"Kiss me," she whispers. "Kiss me like you kiss Neil."

I bend over and put my lips on hers, and her eyes flutter and close, and I kiss her the way Neil told me he likes it, long and full, and Vanessa kisses back. It could be she imagines this person in the hat and suit she is kissing is Eddie Grandinetti or a groom in a black tuxedo or a kid who won't go to the prom because he won't get the courage up to ask anyone. But I am just kissing Vanessa.

Acetate

1

Nell and Drummond and Crystal, the three of them, lived in Colorado, in a house they rented near the state university.

Then Drummond said he was going to graduate school on the East Coast, where he would get a degree in creative writing and become a little famous.

Then Nell got pregnant.

There were places to get an abortion in Fort Collins, but Nell wanted to go to Boulder, where they would give you an abortion by placing seaweed at the entrance of your cervix. This was in the early eighties, when people had taken to standing outside clinics and singing "Amazing Grace" and waving the enlarged photos of fetuses in formaldehyde.

"And I am not putting up with any of that crud," Nell said.

Crystal said she would be happy to go with Nell to Boulder, but Nell said that wouldn't be necessary, Drummond was going to take her. In Crystal's opinion, Drummond didn't seem like the sort of person who could be relied upon to act properly in a difficult situation.

Only emergencies brought out good qualities in Drummond. If you fell down a flight of stairs and ended up with a bone poking through your skin, or if you managed foolishly to set your hair on fire while cooking dinner, Drummond was the sort of person who could be counted on to treat you for shock while you waited for the ambulance to arrive; also the one who would roll you up in a rug to smother the flames. But Drummond was not so good at long, dragged-out crises.

The day of the abortion itself appealed to him somewhat, as this involved transporting a patient to and from a medical facility. But by the time that day finally arrived, he was bored. He had gotten bored way back, between the day Nell did the pregnancy test and the day she called to schedule the abortion. He didn't really want to hear about how crummy Nell felt and how she could only eat saltines. He didn't want to hear anything about seaweed or cervixes.

"For all the good it did us, you might as well have let me go in without the armor," he said. *Armor,* Drummond's word for condoms. He helped Nell climb into the cab of his truck. Crystal had prepared a duffel bag with a change of underwear and sanitary napkins and some hand towels in case Nell had to throw up; also the ubiquitous sleeve of saltines. Nell wore Crystal's rose quartz earrings that were said to be calming to the nervous system.

"I don't think she'll be comfortable in the truck," Crystal said. Since getting pregnant, Nell liked to lie down at certain moments and pull her legs into her chest. This would be difficult in a truck. "You can take Sojourner," Crystal said. Her old Toyota wagon was so reliable it had a name. Nell had festooned the dashboard and the odd shelf beneath the glove compartment with bits of sea glass and totemic rocks from Scotland and the Oregon coast, where if you placed your hand on the mussels growing on the surface of a giant rock, you could feel all of them living and pulsing when they shrank away from your hand.

The name, the totemic rocks. They drove Drummond crazy.

Drummond said he hated driving an automatic, and Nell said she would do just fine in the truck. She was looking brave. With

Crystal's help, she had selected an outfit the previous night: a corduroy jumper Nell described as the color of sea foam along with a plaid shirt shot through with green thread the same color as the jumper. Then brown stockings and leather ankle boots that had zippers up the side. Hers were brown and Crystal's were black: ordering them out of the J. Crew catalogue was the first thing they had done after Nell's pregnancy test came up positive and she got tired of crying. Crystal had said they could drink Drummond's bottle of Merlot that was sitting on top of the refrigerator, but Nell said you weren't supposed to drink when you were pregnant and that Drummond would be angry if they drank his only bottle of Merlot.

"You're only not supposed to drink if you want to *keep* the baby. It doesn't matter if you're aborting."

"Oh God, don't use that word like that. 'Abortion' is bad enough," Nell said.

They drank the wine. They got out the J. Crew catalogue.

❖ ❖ ❖

Neither of them had any money. They were putting themselves through college on loans and babysitting jobs. Nell did some sewing for people; she had taught herself how to sew when she was in grade school. She had been born in the States, but her father had moved them back to his hometown in western Canada while Nell was still a baby. Then her father died young in an electrical accident while working for the phone company. An electrical *incident*, Nell called it. She felt that "accident" unnecessarily placed blame on her father. Afterward, she and her mother were supposed to move back to the States, but her mother became an alcoholic and lost interest in everything but gardening and vodka. This part Nell didn't mention to Drummond, though she told him that her mother cultivated fabulous gardens. She grew clematis and delphiniums and cosmos; also vegetables that rotted on the vine unless Nell went out and collected them in a bowl.

Nell and Drummond agreed that each of them would pay for half the abortion. This business with the seaweed cost more money than an ordinary abortion, but Nell could not be budged from the idea.

The woman who fetched Nell from the waiting room had a nametag on her jacket lapel that said "Candy." Right away, Drummond stood up and said he wanted to be with Nell throughout the abortion, as he was the father. Nell thought she saw Candy's lips twitch when he said that word, but maybe it was only because Drummond said "abortion" and "father" so loudly in an office containing other women who were most likely also at the office to obtain abortions.

"Candy," Drummond said, when the three of them got into an office with Candy sitting on one side of the desk and Drummond and Nell on the other. "That's a great name for a nurse."

"The nurse, I'm sure, will be interested to hear that," Candy said.

Already these antagonisms, with Nell in the middle of them.

Candy explained what Nell should expect at each stage of the procedure and afterward. From his breast pocket Drummond extracted a small notepad.

❖ ❖ ❖

Nell was standing outside in a burgundy satin bathrobe she'd bought with Drummond in mind, as he had once mentioned that he disliked her plaid woodsy clothes. But the satin went cold immediately and chilled her, so that she'd had to go in and get her parka to put over it. Drummond was trying to tie his bicycle to the back of his truck. It was several days since the abortion, but Nell was still bleeding; the sanitary pads she changed every couple of hours like giant soggy bricks caught between her legs. She would have liked Drummond to postpone the drive to Virginia, but his graduate program was starting in four days. He had apologized to Nell. He hadn't planned on her getting pregnant right before he was all set to go to graduate school. He'd had his plans set months earlier, back in mid-March. They had been using armor.

"If you're going to break up with me, I'd rather you do it now," Nell said. An early frost on the grass bent and crunched under the wood heels of her clogs. "We could make a clean break and you could put some miles between us and make it clean between us." She held up her hands and made a gesture of breaking a stick and holding a piece in each hand.

Drummond was having trouble getting the bicycle properly installed in the rack. "Shit," he said.

"I wouldn't be mad if it happened now. Whereas if you go all the way to Virginia and meet someone else and then break up with me, *that* would make me mad."

There are the times when women believe such conversations are necessary, to mark out the dimensions of a moment. Departures, reunions, anniversaries. The departures and reunions themselves, the actual events, must be imprinted with this kind of talk in order to be considered true departures, real reunions.

"I can't get this damn thing to sit properly in the rack," Drummond said.

Crystal was crouching in her bedroom by the window tucked just under the roof, with her forehead against the screen. The grid of the screen was starting to agitate the skin on her forehead, but if she pulled back it was harder for her to hear. She could hear most of what Drummond was saying and hardly any of Nell, who was soft-spoken not as a biological consequence of being a diminutive woman but by virtue of her nationality. (All the Canadians Crystal had ever met were soft-spoken and, by comparison with Americans, refreshingly equivocal. It would have surprised her to hear Nell requesting the courtesy of a clean break from Drummond.)

"Are you listening to me, Drummond?"

"I am not breaking up with you, Nell. Not here and not in Virginia."

2

Crystal and Nell were painting the New York City skyline on large mural sheets of white paper tacked to their living room wall. This was months after Drummond left for Virginia.

Nell had a letter from Drummond. She still got letters nearly every week.

"There are moments when I think about what could have been with our child. I think of how he would be speaking. I would teach him to say my name. Drum. That is what I would have liked to have been his first word."

A UPS man came to the door with a package.

"It's probably fine," Nell said. She held the package against her chest and pressed at the contents. "It just feels like clothes."

It was a sweater set, from J. Crew. Drummond was good at pulling off these sorts of moves.

"Dusk," Nell said. "It has the buttons I like."

Not just buttons. *Pearlized shank buttons.* Nell could have recited its features from memory. *Pure merino wool in a very fine rib stitch. Mesh ribbon trim at the placket. Overwashed for softness. Imported.*

"It looks like he got me a small," she said doubtfully. She was already taking off the tee shirt of Drummond's she was wearing. It was gray and had the word *inmate* printed across the back of it in black capital letters.

"He knows nothing about child development," Crystal said. "Children don't even begin forming recognizable words until they're a year old."

"Probably he has a fantasy that his would have been precocious, since he's a writer," Nell said. In front of the mirror she was appraising herself. "I don't know that I would ordinarily choose dusk," she said.

"Your baby would not have been speaking. It would just barely have been born."

Nell turned from the mirror. "Oh, don't say that."

The skyline Nell and Crystal were painting was for Alma. She had moved into the bedroom that Drummond had vacated. Her mouth at all times stayed slightly open, which reminded Crystal of a door left ajar for purposeful but obscure reasons. It seemed as if Alma was always waiting for the possibility of seduction or conversation, maybe both. Maybe both were the same, for Alma. If Nell or Crystal walked into the room, she jumped up from what she was doing and barraged them with ordinary questions and facts. The bus was late. Her hair got caught in a door hinge and a Cute Boy disentangled it (all good-looking men were Cute Boys). She was going to be reading at open-mike night at The Stone Lion, the local bookstore. Like Drummond, Alma was a writer who worked at Coopersmith's Brew Pub. Drummond had put her in contact with Nell and Crystal when he moved out. "She's a little conceited, but she's not too emotionally fucked up or in therapy or anything," Drummond had said.

Alma was attractive and Chinese and persecuted, for being attractive and Chinese. Also for her height. She was six feet tall.

❖ ❖ ❖

Drummond sent lots of gifts from Virginia. He sent the long, dry seed pods that fall off the catalpa trees in autumn in Virginia. He sent a large art book about Frida Kahlo, Nell's favorite artist. He sent a dead bee (Emily Dickinson had once sent a dead bee to a correspondent, along with a poem, Drummond said: he was full of this sort of literary lore), sublingual vitamin B-12 lozenges, a recipe for a vegan cheesecake he had eaten in a country inn that he thought Nell would like (he had gone into the kitchen and wangled the recipe out of the pastry chef). He sent a photo of himself shirtless and writing at a desk. Crystal did not think that Drummond had the sort of physique that did itself any favors by being photographed shirtless. He had an alarmingly narrow chest, and veiny white arms that managed somehow to seem both strong and sickly.

"Look at what he says after the baby's first word thing." Nell, after some months of pining silently, had gotten into the habit of showing Crystal parts of the letters, or at least parts of some of them. Maybe there were others that Nell kept entirely to herself.

Crystal read the sentence Nell was pointing to. *"I have been thinking of how I would have liked to name him Conrad."*

"There was never one conversation about keeping any baby," Nell said. "We never even used that kind of terminology."

"Why Conrad?"

The skin on Nell's face pulled back and tightened. "I know there must be instructional films or something that show couples deliberating about whether to have an abortion or keep the baby, but that wasn't Drum and me. I didn't want it and neither did he. We were using birth control. Birth control doesn't work a hundred percent of the time, but we tried. Now all of a sudden it's a baby and then it's a boy and then he's got a name for it."

Nell hadn't told Drummond about the phone calls or the objects left on the front porch. A package from UPS had arrived that she thought was from J. Crew and tore open with her usual enthusiasm for UPS packages. It contained a cloth rag doll soaked in a fluid resembling blood. And then sometimes Crystal or Nell picked up the phone and the voice on the other end—a male voice—asked if she was regretting having killed her baby.

Crystal thought Nell should tell Drummond about these incidents.

"It would just make it worse."

❖ ❖ ❖

Alma had made it clear that she was expecting some sort of dramatic recognition of her birthday. She was loudly homesick. It was Nell who suggested to Crystal that they paint the New York skyline for her and then have a cocktail party in the middle of it. Crystal was so pleased to hear Nell come up with a social idea after months of being depressed by Drummond's leaving that she agreed instantly to the project, without realizing how much time and effort were going to be involved.

Really, the idea for the skyline and the cocktail party had been Alma's; she had hinted at it several times to Nell when Crystal wasn't around. Alma was the sort of person who believed that roommates should do small, thoughtful things for each other. She left sticks of gum or pieces of hard candy on Nell's and Crystal's pillows, both bathrooms were stocked with strongly floral-scented soaps that Nell apologized for not using because her skin could only tolerate hypoallergenic soaps and Crystal apologized for not using because she did not like strongly floral-scented soaps, and Alma had purchased two appliances that she announced were "for the house": an espresso maker and a salad spinner.

❖❖❖

For her birthday party, Alma got herself up in a matching violet rayon top and skirt designed in such a way to show her belly, brown and appealingly not quite flat.

"She's not even thin, exactly. She's not in shape. And those pockmarks on her face. She must have had bad acne as a teenager." Nell and Crystal were hiding out in the kitchen, away from the other guests, most of them friends of Alma's from Coopersmith's or from a writer's group Drummond had held at the house a few times. The party was just beginning to collapse into noise and social risk-taking. People were getting drunk enough to start wandering off and opening doors clearly meant to remain closed to partygoers; soon, people would trickle into the kitchen and start scavenging for additional snacks and booze in the refrigerator and cupboards. They would be hunting down Oreos, Baileys Irish cream, a pint of Häagen Dazs. Things you swore, in the clear light of sobriety, you would never eat. The cheese and crackers and chips put out on the dining room table for the guests wouldn't be sufficient. They never were.

"Men don't even seem to like her very much," Nell said. "It's that she likes herself so much that it doesn't matter."

"She covered the pockmarks with makeup," Crystal said.

"A lot of it."

"That takes guts."

"I bet Alma would like to have a photo taken of herself at a writing desk."

"With no shirt on."

They were both a little drunk on a bottle of wine they had started on before the guests arrived.

In the living room, in front of New York City (Nell and Crystal's cockeyed representation of it, with the Empire State Building uptown from the Citicorp Building), Alma was telling people about her novel. She was writing a novel about growing up Chinese in New York City.

"The mean streets," one of the guests said. Nell had recognized him earlier as one of the writers with whom Drummond had been competitive. It seemed to her that Drummond might have called him some funny name, way back when. A cliché monger. He said it the way Alma said "Cute Boy," with emphasis. Cliché Monger. *Monga*, he said.

"Triumph over adversity," Monga shouted. People were in general communicating by way of shouting at this point in the party.

"I'll just read you this one little bit," Alma said, and dashed off to get her journal upstairs. She believed that first drafts of novels should be written in clothbound journals.

On the way up to her bedroom, Alma paused and kissed Crystal and then Nell, once on the forehead for each of them. "You think it's okay I'm reading to them?" she asked. In her violet outfit, with a roll of skin pushing out above the waist and her long black hair cut straight in bangs across her forehead, and in her smeared dark purple lipstick and with the red wine staining her teeth a violety blue, she looked to Nell like a harem girl.

"I'm sure they'll love you reading to them," Crystal said.

"I guess *harem girl's* not politically correct," Nell said, when

Alma was on her way up the stairs. The truth was that she did not like Alma very much; also that it bothered her that she had no rational reason not to like Alma, who was kind and complimentary and always giving her little presents.

Crystal laughed. "You don't have to speak every little thought that comes into your head. It probably wouldn't kill you not to say it, even if you're thinking it."

Nell considered this. While considering, she foraged in the cabinet above the sink and located a box of pretzels.

The passage Alma read from her novel concerned a very beautiful woman in a major American city talking to her wise grandmother from the old country about the number of men pursuing her. Every night she called her grandmother to discuss her man trouble. The chapter from which the passage came, in fact, was called "Man Trouble." The beautiful woman was not pleased with the devastating effect she had on men, mainly because their admiration got perverted by their interest in her ancestry. Alma stood in front of the skyline mural and read by the light of a candle held by Monga, who was swayingly drunk and concentrating hard on holding the candle steady.

❖ ❖ ❖

"There was clapping after that, I think," Crystal said. It was about the only sentence she and Nell could piece together the morning after the party, in the Silver Grille Café, where they were nursing their wine headaches with cups of coffee and large, cakey muffins. They had a midterm the next day in women's studies, the one class they took together. The title of their textbook, *Major Problems in American Women's History,* threw Crystal off whenever she ran through it in her head. It had a discomfiting ambiguity, as if in some way American women's history itself was a problem.

They were reviewing chapter 6, "The Family Lives of Enslaved Women."

In Tudor and Stuart England, men were fully accustomed to disease and a low expectation of life. Parents were slower to recognize the individuality of their children, for they well knew that they might lose them in their infancy. Nobody thought, as we ordinarily think today, that every child already contained a man's personality. Too many of them died.

"I think she liked the party," Nell said.
"She liked reading to everyone the best."
"That's writers for you," Nell said.

Women who did not want children knew how to abort or to arrange to have a child die soon after birth. With childbirth deaths so common from natural causes, the deed could not be easily detected.

"The *deed*," Nell said, drawing out the word.

3

Drummond had known right from the first that the woman—Candy, with the purple pants and the saltwater taffy that got stuck in his teeth—was the doctor, not the nurse. It wasn't even that he wanted to let her know that he was capable of taking her down a notch, though probably that was what Nell thought he was up to. What he had needed to see was the doctor's reaction. Maybe she would be angry or sarcastic, maybe she would ignore him entirely or correct him with a strained politeness. You couldn't always trust your own speculation; sometimes you had to test out a hypothesis. There was one time when he was thinking about a male character who took an almost anthropological, or at the very least an exaggeratedly physiological, interest in women's bodies. This character was interested, for instance, in the different shapes of the vagina. Drummond got to asking women he dated if he could take a look at their vaginas and then touch them, at first, with the same objective disinterest with which a gynecologist examines a vagina. But you could not always anticipate the range of reactions such a request might produce. Nell's he had anticipated. The coyness, the melting and yielding. But Alma had been another story altogether. Two possible reactions he had anticipated were outrage and embarrassment. Alma, though, had not gone near either of these. She had not understood.

They had left work after their shifts ended and gone to her apartment, the duplex she lived in before she moved in with Nell and Crystal. It was late in the afternoon, a weekday. Alma knew he had a girlfriend—she might even have met Nell once or twice, at the restaurant—but she was up for it anyway. Just a fling, she called it. She said a fling was when two friends fooled around and then still liked each other just as much afterward and didn't require anything more than friendship from each other.

"We're friends, but you're so pretty," he told her. He really did think this; it wasn't an effort to sound sincere. She had the shiniest black hair he had ever seen on someone not on television and a plump mound of a belly that sat unexpectedly in the section of her below firm breasts and above taut thighs that crossed and uncrossed while they talked.

He sat down next to her on the bed. She had a coverlet made of a magenta satiny material with cream-colored crescent moons sewn on it. All around the room were photos of Alma with her large family or of her alone with her grandmother, a stooped woman who looked like a dwarf standing beside Alma.

"You're very tall," Drummond said. He was dismayed to feel his penis getting hard, as he had meant for all this to be a research project that would turn into passion only by him willing it to.

"*You* are very tall," Alma said. "We match up." She was leaning against him in a black turtleneck sweater that was too tight for her. "Will you kiss me, Drummond? For the longest time I've wanted to know what it would be like for you to kiss me."

Then he was kissing her, with his penis hard in his pants, and he did not have a chance to do much in the way of holding a hand between her legs and telling her she had a lovely vagina. Alma had other ideas. She wanted to pose for him, in the manner of centerfold models in pornographic magazines. She drizzled some sort of oil on her breasts and arranged herself on the magenta coverlet.

"Take a picture. See the camera, over there?"

He lifted the camera off her dresser. It was one of the complicated ones used by people who know something about photography. He fiddled with the lens in a way that he hoped made him look legitimate.

"This doesn't even look like it has any film in it."

"It doesn't matter. You can still be the photographer."

4

All the bus stops near the university had benches printed with advertisements of services and products of interest to students. Duds and Suds, the laundromat that served beer, had a bench, as did Coopersmith's and The Stone Lion Bookstore. The bench at the intersection of University Drive and College Avenue had an advertisement that asked, "Injured By Abortion?" There was a phone number to call to get legal representation for your case.

It was Crystal's idea that they should buy spray paints and fix that advertisement. They would go out under cover of night on their bicycles.

They might need fortification. She made up a batch of margaritas and filled a thermos for each of them—strong, because the thermoses were not that big. She told Nell they should probably wear dark clothes and hats, so that people would not spot them.

"What are you two kooks doing?" Alma asked, when she saw them with the thermoses and the dark clothes.

"Just going out for a bike ride," Nell said.

"At this hour?"

"The pollution has all settled by now." Nell said this with the superior authority of a scientist who points out obvious facts about the physical world fully obscured from view until the scientist all in one stroke reveals them. Crystal had a feeling Alma might object to the project of altering the advertisement.

Alma wagged a finger at them. "I think you two are up to something."

On their bicycles, they rode through City Park, Nell taking the lead on the narrower paths to help Crystal, who was not a confident cyclist.

"Ain't I a woman," Crystal called out to the shape of Nell ahead of her, outfitted in black but topped with a white blot of a helmet. Nell didn't call anything back; she didn't take up the thread of what Crystal was giving her.

At the edge of the park, they dismounted their bicycles and walked them across College Avenue.

They laid their bicycles at the edge of a thicket of trees and walked to the curb, neither of them saying anything. Crystal's adrenaline was making things inside her—heart, thoughts, blood—race. She had gone to a couple of pro-choice rallies, but she had never done anything radical in service of a political belief. She would not have thought to paint the bench if Nell hadn't been getting sinister packages and phone calls. A great deafening wave of history was cresting over them; that was how it felt to Crystal.

"Do you think we could sit here for a second and drink the margaritas?" Nell asked.

Nell drank hers too quickly, gulping as if it were bottled water. When Crystal saw that, she gulped hers too, thinking that would get them walking to the bench more quickly. But that didn't happen; Nell sat with her empty thermos in her hand and began moaning. The sounds were incoherent for a while, then changed to words.

"I found a picture of him. In with her stuff."

It took Crystal a long time to get out of Nell what the picture was and whose stuff it was with and what stuff it was.

"You know that magenta thing she has on her bed? The throw with the moons? He's got that draped over him."

❖❖❖

"Dear Drummond," Crystal said.

They were sitting on Crystal's bed. Later now, more margaritas. Nell had the notebook in her lap.

"I can't," Nell said.

"Dear Drummond. That much you can write."

Like you, I have changed somewhat in my views in the past year. A friend gave me a book, The Handbook on Abortion. *The pictures shocked me. I did not know that what got taken out of me looked like that, a real baby with a head and little toes and fingers that can wave. I just pictured it as a cluster of cells, that early on. But it looks like I was wrong.*

"I don't know about the fingers that can wave part," Crystal said.

"I was going to put in something about buying a toy drum," Nell said.

"He would eat that up. But maybe you should save it for the next letter."

5

Crystal was home from work with the flu when she saw the review in the *San Francisco Chronicle*. After that, she couldn't help keeping an eye out for it in the *New York Times* and the other major dailies. She searched on the Internet and found reviews of the book that praised its "darkly realistic vision of the underbelly of modern American life." Also its "finely detailed account of a man's anguish at losing his child to an abortion."

She called Nell in Salt Lake City, where she lived with her husband and helped him run a bicycle shop.

"Listen to this," she shouted into the phone. She had not known she would be so enraged and interested.

It was fine, Nell said. Drummond's vision involved serious inroads into sentimental claptrap. The female character's emotions about her imaginary, thwarted baby would be all wrong. It didn't matter if everyone bought it.

Then Nell remembered something and burst out laughing. "He was very timid when I first met him," she said. "Did I ever tell you this? He would do things to me and act as if he was only doing them if I gave him permission. 'Look at your lovely little breasts,' he would say. 'You want me to touch them?' Well, what could I say?

"He would touch me in this way like he was reluctant. Like he knew I had TB or something and would probably give it to him, but he was going to take the risk anyway, for *my* sake. He'd get me to take off my pants and underwear in the same way, and he'd sit there with all his clothes still on looking at me. One night when we were sitting on my bed and he'd gotten me naked, he asked me if I'd like to put my legs up, and he put his hand between my legs, a few inches from my crotch. Like a photographer does, setting up a shot. 'Your lovely vagina,' he says. Just like that. 'Your lovely vagina.' Like he was going to do an anatomical drawing of a vagina and as luck would have it I happened to have a very good specimen."

No one had ever said anything to Crystal, plus or minus, about her vagina.

"Of course, *that* was the beginning of the end," Nell said.

6

During the abortion procedure, the necessity of lying on her back made Nell hiccup through tears with a force she had not expected. It was a great surprise to her to find out she believed, in spite of the fact that she was pro-choice and had already decided she did not want children, that an irreplaceable portion of her life's energy was being sucked out of her. She would never be able to get it back. A stretch of time went by, impossible to determine how long, when she absented herself from her body. She went somewhere else. Her town in Canada came to her, and her mother in a tulip-covered housedress with a trowel and filth on her hands, though a nice filth. Then a moleskin tuxedo skirt she wanted from the J. Crew catalogue: *contrast satin trim at waist, dyed-to-match tuxedo braid at side seams. Fully lined in acetate.* "Acetate" always made her think of how certain things were flammable. It went like this for a while, Nell thinking of Canada and her mother and acetate. Later she would remember or at least describe this to Crystal as a moment of transcendence, but at the time it just felt like something necessary and expedient to do when medical personnel were putting metal apparatus up inside of you. Candy was wearing pants that looked to be made of a purple silk material. Nell could see them through the *V* her legs made.

"Are we doing all right there?" Candy said.

Nell said yes, and then went even further away, though she was still able to answer "yes" each time Candy asked. She had not anticipated the noise the machines made, a whirring that would have prompted from her mother a familiar phrase. She could see her mother standing in the backyard with the clear mug she liked filled halfway with tea and holding the mug out in the direction of the neighbors' yard, as the neighbors had a motorized lawn mower that did not meet with her approval.

Person can't hear herself think, with all that noise.

It felt that way with Drummond sometimes—as if he was making all sorts of noise and mayhem. Now, for instance. She arrived back at herself and in the room, with recognizable corners and surfaces. Candy was through with her. The machine or the several machines were not making noise anymore. Drummond was talking with Candy. Another nurse had hold of her arm and was explaining again what she might expect her body to do and feel in the next forty-eight hours.

"God no, that's a pediatric rectal," Candy was saying. "That one there is the one I used on Nell. A Pederson."

"A Peterson? With a *t*?"

"A *d*. Not the Pederson virginal. See the skinny one there? That's only for virgins, because—obviously—the regular Pederson is much too wide. That widest one is a Graves."

Afterward, in Candy's office, Nell noticed a glass jar with CANDY painted on it in jumbled letters.

"People are always giving me candy and candy accessories," Candy said. "It's lucky my name isn't Chastity, right?" She offered them the jar and Drummond took a piece of saltwater taffy and Nell took a green sour ball. The taffy got caught in Drummond's teeth, so that he had to try unobtrusively to loosen it with a finger while carrying on the conversation. He was still taking notes, probably on how much pain reliever to give Nell and what to do if she began hemorrhaging.

On the way home in the truck, Drummond was cheerful and talkative. "Well, I bet you're relieved that's over. How do you feel?" he asked.

Until that moment, Nell would have thought there was nothing she would have liked more than to be asked that question. But then, when he did, she told him she was fine.

Lovely

I have been in Ireland ten days. I left a child back in New York, but he is Elvin's. Sure, he came out of me, I'm his real mother, but he was Elvin's boy from the start. Same small ears pressed flat against their skulls, same preoccupation with how the world works rather than who's in it. Elvin and Danny spend Saturday afternoons playing with gyroscopes or wandering through the Museum of Natural History, where they can stare at the bones of dinosaurs. Danny is not yet convinced they're extinct.

I used to take tickets at the Angelika theater in NoHo. One sunny summer day I came across a battered book of Edna O'Brien's short stories in the coatroom and read a story called "A Scandalous Woman." The last line calls Ireland "a land of strange, throttled, sacrificial women." Trapped in my booth with nothing to look at but the dilapidated Pineapple Health Club across the street, a box of Milk Duds and a cup of espresso my only sustenance for the seven remaining hours of my shift, I put my head down on my folded arms and sobbed. I was still sniffling when customers started lining up for the next show, and my supervisor finally told me to go pull myself together. I walked to Midtown and booked a flight to Ireland. Manhattan seemed a place utterly indifferent to throttled, sacrificial women. In fact, the women themselves, striding along the sidewalk with their sunglasses and black clothes, with their arrogant chins, radiated a bright, impenetrable halo of indifference. I wanted to go to a place teeming with throttled women, to hang my suffering on a hook among others.

❖❖❖

My first full day in Dublin, Dunkin' Donuts had its grand opening. There was a long line outside. As I walked past, I caught a glimpse of a certain kind of doughnut with pink icing that Elvin and Danny can't keep away from. Below the statue of Padraig O'Connell, a little girl was feeding part of her doughnut to some birds. An older boy shouted, "Don't waste it on scavengers."

I walked in Dublin all day, back and forth across the River Liffey, in and out of bookstores, on the campus of Trinity College. I came across a tourist attraction called "The Viking Experience" and stepped along with ten or twelve other tourists into what appeared to be an elevator. Most of the tourists were mothers with children; I was the only woman whose clothes weren't being tugged. The fake elevator was supposed to give the illusion of being in a time machine. Red digital numbers on a display screen above the doors sped back to the year 988, when Dublin was Dubh Linn, the Black Pool.

When the doors opened again, there was a foul smell of urine and standing pools and decay. Water dripped from the ceiling. The floor beneath us was spongy in some places, solid as stone in others. A man in patched-together furs led us through thatched huts where other actors dressed in period costumes made clothes, cooked food, and built dwellings. They bullied us with questions about our strange clothes, our homes, the plastic gun one boy kept pretending to shoot. They offered a murky stew from a dirty wooden spoon. The children hid behind their mothers' legs while the adults laughed and shook their heads.

In one half-finished hut a man asked me my name. He had

the perfect job for me, he said, then handed me a bucket of manure. When another man warned him to marry someone from his own village, he laughed and said, "Well, maybe not, if Paige'll be around." As I went to join up with my group again, the manure man leaned over and whispered in my ear, "I'll be waitin' for yuh, Paige."

❖❖❖

Elvin and I met in Pittsburgh, where Elvin was doing graduate work at Carnegie Mellon and I was putting myself through Pitt. Three nights a week I cooked at the only health food restaurant in town, a place owned by two brothers from New Delhi. It was called Health Garden, but all of us, even the owners, called it Vindaloo Ghetto. We never had enough hot water or dishes, and the younger brother never let us throw anything away until it began to smell bad. We were arguing over a pot of carrot soup that had taken on a decidedly brown tinge when Elvin stumbled in, looking for a Coke. He took off his knapsack and tapped a cigarette on the back of his hand while I explained to him that we didn't carry Coke, only natural sodas.

"Want to go get a Coke with me?" he asked.

I was working, I said, I couldn't leave the restaurant.

"Oh." He cocked his head and gave me a crooked smile. "You got a match?"

That's Elvin. He'd go looking for a bathroom and stumble into someone's wedding reception.

"You can't smoke in here." I handed him a lemon-lime spritzer.

"No Coke, no smoke." He had a set of tiny teeth nearly as wide as they were long. Many people get teeth like that from grinding them in their sleep. Not Elvin. He sleeps with his mouth wide open, as if in utter stupefaction. A passion for theoretical physics can do that to you. In the evenings, when I came home from work, he'd be doing problem sets on a yellow legal pad, his elbows anchoring loose sheets of paper covered with penciled calculations.

"Say it isn't so, Elv." I'd lean over him and hook my arms around his waist.

"It isn't." He would turn his head to kiss me, then take a peanut and throw it high in the air to see if he could catch it in his mouth before I snatched it.

"So the universe isn't expanding?"

"No. In fact it's contracting, getting smaller and smaller. Finally it'll fold in on itself and disappear. Poof." He took a handful of peanuts, stuffed them in his mouth, and showed me his empty palms.

"No, really," I said. "Expanding or contracting?"

After Danny was born, I didn't need to ask that question anymore.

❖ ❖ ❖

I spent my second evening in Dublin at the Harp Bar. It wasn't as I'd imagined. No pictures of craggy white-bearded bards on the walls, no rough rickety tables that tottered at a touch, no men swaying and slicing at fiddles or thumping homemade bodhrans and singing sad ballads in clipped cadences. A neon harp broad as a bicycle wheel blazed greenly in the plate glass window. Inside: a plush carpet the color of dried blood, American rock music pumping so loud it made my heart hurt, couples shuffling drunkenly under a glittery revolving ball that reminded me of mica. I drank several glasses of Guinness and met an Irishman. We danced; he invited me back to his room at the hotel out by the airport.

He walked backward down O'Connell Street, his hand out to hail a cab. "Clearly you're still in the dark ages," I said. We were having an entirely too jovial conversation about divorce and abortion. Each of us thought we were humoring the other. In the pub, he had invented a charmingly hypothetical scene of passion between us, whispered it in my ear. Now we would go enact it. Yet he had made no mention of birth control. They never do.

We drank a cloudy yellow drink in the hotel pub. Several florid old men sitting at two tables pushed together made bawdy comments about my looks. The wet weather had coiled my hair into silvery blonde ringlets, and my color was high from nerves and all the glasses of stout. There is nothing Irish men like better than a girl with good skin and fair hair. We're the wanton nursemaids, the fairies in the field. One man with jowls that shook kept trying to play a tuba, but he didn't have enough breath. Another stood up to make a toast and knocked over a potted plant.

We went back to his hotel room. There was a roommate— they had been flown up from Cork for a soccer tournament—but he assured me the roommate would be out late drinking. I saw him scribble a note and stick it to the door, but I did not see what it said. I imagined it was very discreet.

He had scabs on his hips from playing soccer. I had never seen a scab on a hip. He wanted to know if I "trained." He chain-smoked in bed. When he turned out the light, all I could see of him was the bright orange tip of his cigarette. It moved and swirled in the dark when he spoke. After he unhooked my bra clasp, he switched on the light again and begged me to take a turn around the room. "You're lovely," he said. I told him I had never heard an American man say "lovely," except in utmost sarcasm.

We drank from a bottle of Paddy Irish whiskey until the green and blue and yellow and red map of Ireland on the label of the bottle blurred. Neither of us said a word about wedding rings, which we were both wearing. The next morning, I sat naked in bed and drank coffee while he retched in the bathroom. "You Catholics," I said when he stumbled out, pale and trembling. "You always make sure you pay for your sins."

I thought we might take a shower together, but in the gray light of morning he showed a misplaced streak of morality. I showered alone. A plastic box on the shower wall dispensed a green liquid that smelled of sulfur. The soap was meant to be used for hair as well as skin. It hardly lathered at all. I wished I hadn't left all my toiletries back at the youth hostel.

Before I left, I helped him into his soccer uniform. His roommate showed up and drank the last of the whiskey. "So, you chatted up a Yank," he said to my lover, who was heading for the bathroom again.

We left the roommate and took a walk out behind the hotel. The grass was overgrown and smelled like rain. He gave me a key chain with a Swiss flag on it. He had played in a tournament against a Swiss team. I wished it was an Irish flag but did not say anything. It was understood that we would not trade addresses. He called a cab, then handed me a five-pound note as I was climbing into the car.

❖ ❖ ❖

A man in a milk truck picked me up hitchhiking five miles outside Dublin. He left liters of milk on top of everyone's privet hedge as we drove along. I stuck my head out the window and looked back at the little white blurs trembling on those green hedge walls. How I would have liked to live in such a place. How simple it seemed, compared to the dizzying, dirty grid of Manhattan.

We stopped at a little pub next to a gas station. Six men were there, in the middle of the day. No women. They asked me a lot of questions about what a girl like me was doing hitchhiking around the country by herself. Thought I was joking when I said the Irish were some of the nicest people I'd ever met. One teetering old man started singing "She Moved through the Fair," and they all made me dance with him. He told me I looked like the female lead in *The Quiet Man,* with John Wayne. I stepped on his toes, apologized, stepped on them again.

The milk truck driver's name was John Joe. He was trying to quit smoking, and there were sourball wrappers all over the dashboard. When I refused a lemon drop, he tossed the whole bag of candy into his glove compartment and grabbed his lighter. I told him I had a husband who smoked in bed. Also, I thought, an Irish lover. "I always have to take the lighter out of his night table," I said. "He could set the damn bed on fire."

"Well," John Joe said, "what's he to do now that you're not there?"

❖ ❖ ❖

I don't have a family. Well, that's not true—I have a family, but we chafed against each other after I got pregnant with Danny, then lost contact. I was one of those people who took all necessary precautions so that I wouldn't get pregnant and got pregnant anyway. Then my parents got uptight and religious all of a sudden, Elvin wanted a baby, and somehow I got talked out of an abortion. Once Danny was born I let Elvin take over. Those nine months did me in.

Elvin is good with children; he sees no barriers between them and adults the way I do. If Danny got fussy in the bathtub, Elvin would shed his own clothes and climb right in. I'd find them splashing and dumping cups of water over each other's heads, their skin wrinkled and soft from staying in the water so long. I'd have to get towels from the hall closet and coax them out, Elvin first and then Danny, into a towel strung between Elvin's outstretched arms.

I decided not to tell John Joe I had a son.

He invited me to stay at his house in Sligo for the night. He lived with just his mother and said she'd be happy for visitors. This she was; when I coughed and blew my nose, she ran off and made hot whiskey with so much sugar in it I could barely manage to get it down.

In the morning John Joe brought me a stack of clean towels. The bathroom was bright green and had pictures of saints on the walls.

Instead of a shower, I drew myself a bath so I could sit and think. I stepped in cautiously, remembering a scare I once had when Danny slipped on the wet tile and chipped one of his front teeth, bloodied his lip. "Just keep him away from mirrors," Elvin whispered to me as he headed out of the bathroom to call the pediatrician. Until Danny got a look at himself and started shrieking, I'd thought Elvin was just tossing off some bit of superstitious foolishness.

After my bath I decided to take a walk around Sligo. I stopped at what looked like a butcher shop. Inside, though, a woodcarver was working. He waved me in. The shop was all gleaming white tile, white floors, white light, like an operating room. Lots of counter space, for cutting meat, I imagine. At one time it must have been quite bloody. But there was no meat anymore, only tree trunks and stumps lying in heaps on the floor, a fine layer of wood shavings over everything.

The woodcarver introduced himself as Roland Quirke. He wore a white smock. I liked watching his pink hands move over the smooth wood. "See this?" He held up a half-finished sculpture of a woman. "This is a piece of ash. Recognize her? Queen Mebh."

He told me a long story about Queen Mebh and a boar on a hill. His cheeks got very red. I picked up a few of the finished carvings and turned them over in my hands. "Hey there," he said. "See this one?" It was a thick tree stump out of which he was carving the figures of three women. He pointed to each emerging figure with his knife. "The Trinity," he said. "Virgin, mother, crone."

He drew a picture of the nearby mountains on a napkin. There were two big mountains in the foreground and a third, smaller mountain between them. He meant for me to see that they were a woman: breasts and a womb. "Most everything's a phallic symbol," he said. "Except for one thing."

"That's very interesting," I said. I saw also that he meant for me to keep the napkin, so I stuffed it in my pocket.

As I was leaving, he dashed over and touched my arm. A sheaf of gray hair had fallen over one of his eyes. "We Irish," he said, "we're primitive, but not stupid."

Was this a final bid for my affections? What would it be like to climb into bed with a woodcutter? I imagined him wanting to pare me down, change me. Virgin, mother, crone: those would be my choices.

A cluster of children in navy blue school uniforms had gathered on the street corner outside the woodcutter's shop. A girl with shiny brown hair had shed her sweater and untucked her white blouse. The back of it was covered with writing in black Magic Marker. A tall boy was reading the slogans on the blouse to the crowd. "Hey, sexy," he read. This set everyone to tittering.

"It doesn't say that at all," the shiny-haired girl said.

"Oh, it does," said the tall boy.

I wondered if the girl was on her way home in that blouse. Honey, I thought, you're in for it.

I overheard two men saying they were "on the dole." Everyone seemed to be unemployed or on the verge of it. I went back to John Joe's house and had tea and white biscuits and jam with his mother. She said she wrote poetry, then read me a poem called "Mall Quay." It was about dancing and singing and being happy in nature. "We're really a pagan people," she said. I noticed a small wart on her nose.

John Joe was not expected home until seven o'clock. His mother went out to Mass at five. I wandered around the house and looked for something to read. Books seemed to be in short supply. I found the Bible, books of poems by Seamus Heaney and Emily Dickinson, a paperback copy of *I'm Okay, You're Okay*, a book about the concentration camps in Germany, and an old course guide for the University of Ulster. I read a series of Heaney's poems about dead bodies in bogs. Halfway through the book, I fell asleep. I dreamt that Danny was a boy in a bog, preserved for centuries in his overalls and dinosaur sneakers.

John Joe took me to a disco. It reminded me of the States.

There were flashing red lights and black walls, a band that sang "Rockin' Robin" and "Hound Dog." The men called each other "lads." At the end of the evening, the bartenders called out, "Drink up, lads!" and began pulling down a set of wooden bars between themselves and the customers. Every five minutes, they pulled the bars down another inch. Pints of stout continued to pass through the foot of space between the bars and the pub counter.

The band started playing the national anthem. Everyone rose and began singing. An old man tried to stand and fell off his stool. Several of us helped him up. He had jagged, triangular teeth, like a dog.

On the way home, John Joe said, "I'd like to see you with your hair pinned up." I didn't know what to say. He had one of those pine-scented Christmas trees made of cardboard hanging from his rearview mirror. I said I didn't know they had those in Ireland. Big drops of rain spattered the windshield. I told him I thought I should leave the next day.

"I didn't mean anything by what I said about your hair," he said.

"No, no," I said. "It's not that. I should just get going."

He asked me to send a postcard from wherever I ended up.

In the morning I got a ride out of town with an old man wearing a plaid tam. He kept drifting into the breakdown lane. He rambled endlessly in a brogue so thick I was not sure he was speaking English. I started wondering how long my money would hold out. Sending a postcard to Elvin and Danny struck me suddenly as a good idea. They seemed very distant, like an afterimage when someone takes a flash photo.

Then something the old man said sifted through. You American girls, he was saying, you all come over here to have a go with the Irish lads.

There was more talk, there was a monologue. His landlady's seventeen-year-old daughter; no, he hadn't gotten her pregnant once; weren't condoms a great invention, you didn't have to pull out just when it was getting lovely; didn't we women like the men with the big tools, the big knobs, like the black men he'd seen in Galway, all the Irish women liked them; would I let him have the feel, just the feel, he'd treat me like one of his own, just the feel. Did my trousers have a zipper.

His hand crept across my lap. The road spun out ahead of us in bumpy black ribbons. A few farmhouses dotted the hills, very far away. The man wanted me to know that he kept a vial of holy water in his glove compartment, for good luck. Also, a package of condoms. The car rattled into a ravine and came to a halt.

I jumped out of the car and ran. Through a thicket of hawthorn bushes and up onto the road I ran, startling two sheep with bright stains of blue dye on their backs. Better to be dyed, I thought, than branded. In the distance, I saw the gray-blue mountains the woodcutter had drawn on the napkin. They did not look like a woman at all.

Love Is Always This, Love Is Never That

1

I've always daydreamed at weddings. I drift off when the wedding march begins, and by the time I snap back it's all over, the I do's done, the rings exchanged, the flower girl fidgeting, the bride in her blinding white dress newly named, radiant and diminished. So far all of my friends have taken their husbands' names. Taken, I wonder, or received? I come from a family that disdains the white dress, the vows, the veil, the pretentious optimism and myopia of such unions.

It is no surprise to me that from a very young age I dreamed myself into a dress with a bustle at the back, my hands overflowing with dahlias, a row of pearly buttons stippled down my spine. For a coworker's wedding I went to the best hairdresser in town. "Classic or sassy?" she asked. I wanted a little of both. She yanked and tugged with a comb and sprayed a sweet mist from a metal can until my hair felt lacquered and smooth as furniture. My chin tipped up, my hair was so heavy.

At the reception I drank too much and teetered around in my high heels, dancing with anyone, until a friend put me to bed on a spare cot in her hotel room. In the morning my hair looked almost exactly as it had the night before. What a regal head it was, as if I had been the bride. I went into the bathroom and set myself to the task of dismantling it.

In the end, I found forty bobby pins. Each made a ticking sound, like the noise a clock makes for the passing of a second, as it hit the tiled floor. They were nearly an hour coming out; I would have liked to take a match to myself.

2

I did not marry. I had a brief, wretched affair with a married Irishman, an illegal immigrant. Colm and I met at Bread for Life, the health food store where we both worked. On Mondays, when we got produce deliveries, he would set aside a handful of Medjool dates for us. These we would eat in the walk-in freezer, our breath gusting out in white puffs when we laughed. We laughed nervously, often, for no reason at all.

The only time we could see each other alone was early in the morning. We began meeting near the store at 5:30 A.M., an hour before the other employees began showing up. I would park my car in the bank lot across the street and watch for him to come wobbling down the sidewalk on his rickety blue bicycle. Chaste and bulky in our parkas, we'd kiss each other's faces and fingers and ears. He'd tell me about the chops he had eaten for dinner and the TV shows he'd watched and the colic remedy he'd given his daughter in the middle of the night. He did not volunteer these details, but gravely gave me the answers when I asked. I wanted to know everything. That's how it was with him.

One day he didn't show up for work. I worried all through that day and the next. On the third afternoon I was chopping celery with the cook in the deli. The store owners kept running through with clipboards and phone messages and impossible questions. They had no idea how to get along without their stock manager.

"They say he was having an affair," the cook said to me. "Can you imagine? Him?" He had never liked Colm.

"What tangled webs," I said, grateful for cliché, and sliced right into my finger. The sight of my own blood, red and warm, encouraged me. I had been longing for a tangible locus of damage.

3

I've been teaching at a state university in the West for three years. One of my students is being followed by a man in a black coat. Of the fourteen women in my freshman composition class, she is clearly the least attractive. Seven of the women have long blonde hair laced with streaks of red or brown. Truly it looks like flax, toffee candy, sanded wood. Anyone would want to touch it. Other women flit and glitter in short skirts, or put themselves together in that tousled, offhand way women can: faded jeans, an oversized blazer, dusky eye shadow, pale lipstick. This student, though, wears dowdy boat shoes and corduroy pants. On Halloween she came to class with a plastic brooch shaped like a jack-o'-lantern pinned to her turtleneck. Just before Thanksgiving vacation, it was a brooch shaped like a turkey.

"Did you go to the police?" I asked her.

They wouldn't do anything, she said, until they had evidence.

What sort of evidence, I wanted to ask.

The following week, she missed a class. She had never missed one before, and we were winding down toward final exams. That weekend I had a nightmare about her. She was being taunted by a group of fraternity brothers and was thrown down a flight of stairs, only to be hoisted up and thrown down again. The rugby shirts the men wore were specked with blood. When I awoke, I realized the fraternity house in my dream had been one I'd frequented in college. I'd dated one of the brothers, and one night after he'd fallen asleep I'd gotten up and looked in the fraternity's file cabinet. I found a file containing songs for pledges to learn. All the songs were filled with words to describe women that I thought only pimps and pornographers used: that is how naive I was.

I did not wake up my boyfriend and shake the song sheets in his face. I climbed back into bed beside him. For the first time, I noticed that the room smelled musky and close, like sex. It occurred to me that dozens of fraternity brothers and their dates had used my boyfriend's bed. Women I saw every day in class, on the Quad, at the library—we had all writhed in that same groove in the mattress.

My student showed up for the next class. Afterward, we walked to a coffee shop, and she told me about the man in the black coat. She had started carrying a camera with her all the time. One afternoon, her practice with the college band ended early, so she was waiting outside the library for her roommate to pick her up. The man appeared and tried to touch her.

"Does he talk to you?" I asked.

"I tell him to stay away from me," she said, "and sometimes he answers back."

I wanted to ask what he said, but she went on. She had pulled out her camera and tried to take a picture of him. He had panicked and snatched the camera out of her hands. She could dimly recall him smashing it to the ground before he grabbed her and knocked her head against a wall.

The next day she had received half a dozen irises at her dorm room.

4

I was trying to get a second job to supplement my teaching salary when Jack asked me to move in with him, so that's what I did. He lived in a suburb of Denver, with lace curtains and paintings of Nantucket beaches and a wool rug from Ireland that his mother gave him as a gift. It is precisely the color of sheep. In the living room he had chairs that were made by slaves. The chairs were passed down through generations of Jack's family, which at one time owned a plantation in Kentucky. "Can you guess which are copies?" Jack asked. Two were. I couldn't.

Not long after I moved in, I got sick and had to stay in bed for a week. One day Jack was in the bathroom, peeing and singing. I could hear in his voice that he was getting a little tired of bringing me vegetable broth and homeopathic remedies. I was taking bryonia and pulsatilla, for the phlegm and coughing. Also ignatia, for grief. I kept the vial in my pillowcase, so I could toss a capful of pellets under my tongue while he was out of the room. I didn't like to deceive him, but Jack was one of those people who hates unhappiness. "If I were a woman and you were a man, I'd send you roses . . . ," he sang.

His family's plantation is gone now, but in its place is a museum where you can buy souvenirs and see all sorts of things slaves made, on exhibit, behind glass.

"I see what you're getting at," Jack said, when I described the museum that way.

I didn't like having chairs made by slaves in our living room. You couldn't sit on one without thinking about the lash of a whip against a back.

5

I am never glad to return to New York, but I was expected home for the Christmas holidays. Jack and I flew out East together, and he went to see his sister in Boston. My parents have a converted beach house on Long Island. My favorite part of the property is a white gate with an old-fashioned latch. Open the gate and there are worn stone steps leading down to the beach. My friend Hinderly came for my parents' annual Christmas party. I invited him on a dare from my mother, who claims my friends are much more uptight and conservative than hers are. She's right; they are.

When Hinderly and I go out in Manhattan, his neck swivels every time a pretty young woman passes by. We saw one in a lavender linen dress on East Eighty-sixth Street. "Look at that," he whispered. Her posture, he thought, suggested a certain kind of discipline.

"Go see what she's reading," I said. She was carrying a thick paperback book.

"Good idea." He was already running to catch up with her. It's important to Hinderly that women be both pretty and smart. In this he imagines himself a kind of feminist.

In his enthusiastic pursuit, Hinderly almost bumped into a parking meter. He paused to wait for me at the corner.

"What was it?" I asked.

"Some Sidney Sheldon novel." We looked at each other and sniffed.

At my parents' Christmas party, Hinderly drank too much. At first this was not a problem. Drinks tend to make Hinderly more sociable. He had a lengthy conversation with an old friend of my mother's who wears a leather headband with a feather in it that looks like it once belonged to a swan.

After reading aloud an article on the winter solstice that he had clipped from the *Wall Street Journal,* Hinderly put on his coat and helped me into mine. He wanted a walk on the beach. We poured a gray, sticky liqueur into paper cups and headed down the stone stairs behind my house. I was tipsy and chirping about some traveling Jack and I were planning to do. On a narrow path that swung through a patch of swaying cattails, Hinderly grabbed me by my scarf.

"Don't settle," he said. "You'll stifle."

I thought this a cryptic and drunken thing to say. Saliva glistened on his puffy lower lip. We were almost the same height.

Impulsively, he embraced me. His breath smelled of mint and licorice, and for a moment I imagined something benign and pleasant, a penny candy shop out on the east end of Long Island where my parents always let us stop during long car trips out that way. I could see the heavy glass bottles filled with red and black licorice twists, gumdrops shaped like mint leaves and sprinkled with sugar, the pastel pinks and greens of saltwater taffy in twists of crinkly white paper. I imagined Hinderly's childhood filled with solemn, obligatory ceremonies: prep school entrance exams, divorces and remarriages, tea parties given by elderly aunts, cocktail parties through which a tiny replica of the Hinderly who now hugged me trundled in starched white shirts and bright bow ties and shiny black shoes.

Still clasping the ends of my scarf, he laid his head against my shoulder. "I love you," he whispered into the lapels of my wool coat.

He clung to me like a child, then tried to kiss me. I turned away, toward the harbor, and watched the whitecaps rolling across Long Island Sound. Sleet pricked at my face. I remembered my student and the irises her pursuer had sent her.

I started back toward my parents' house. A rectangle of yellow light shone through the sliding glass door. I aimed for that, bending my head against the sleet. Behind me, I heard Hinderly's footsteps. "Wait!" he shouted, his expensive shoes crunching on beach straw. I stumbled toward my house through mud and broken shells left by a tide that had retreated.

6

A student at the university where I teach was abducted in a van. I read this in the newspaper. The story did not give the woman's name. Of course, you can imagine the conclusions I drew. But when I called my student, she picked up the phone right away and reported that the man in the black coat had stopped following her. No more notes, flowers, head bashings.

I remembered our class discussion one day about audiences for essays. Two young women wanted to write their essays on rape, with rapists as their imagined audience.

"You have to write to an audience that will *care,*" one of the young men in the class said. He sat up front and had the alert, blank face of a student leader.

I said, reluctantly, that he had a point.

My student, the one being pursued by the man in the black coat, had been quietly doodling in the margins of her notebook. Suddenly she flared up. "Maybe if we told them how they make us feel!" We all turned and stared at her.

In the end, she did direct her essay toward, in her words, "Men who rape and otherwise violate women." She told about sitting on the toilet in a stall and watching the feet go by. How she was always expecting to see a pair of men's shoes, and how she resorted to getting a friend to accompany her to the bathroom, no matter the hour. Also, how she found herself eating maple walnut fudge and chocolate-covered cherries in bed. Filling herself with things rich and heavy and sweet, she could pretend he wouldn't attack her. How could anyone hurt a girl eating candy under a pink comforter?

7

When summer came, I left Jack and went off to Ireland. It was only when I got there that I realized I hadn't even planned a way to leave the airport. So I walked. On the road to Limerick I found part of a cardboard box in a hedge and tore off a panel. On it I wrote RIDE NEEDED in pencil, working at the letters until they were dark.

A man and his daughter picked me up. He was a solicitor, he said. He was on his way back from fetching her at school. We chatted for a while about the Irish referendum on divorce, which was big in the news at the time, but he seemed to want to tell me something.

"You don't want to be askin' for a ride," he said finally. We had entered Limerick, which looked more busy and glum than I had imagined. I thought a town with such a name would exude an air of whimsy, its inhabitants capering and cheerful.

"Is it dangerous?" I asked the solicitor.

No, he said, tourists usually didn't run into any trouble. Then he explained, in the most roundabout way, that the word *ride* had other meanings. "What you're lookin' for," he said, "is a lift. Ask for a ride and you might get more than you bargained for." He blushed, then gave in to a belly laugh. I laughed with him.

We got some cardboard from a food store, and the little girl sat down on the curb to make me another sign. Her skin was the texture and color of heavy cream, but there was already an adult hardening around the eyes, as if love had been withheld or offered slyly, with conditions. She worked with avid, desperate focus, as if she thought one of us might snatch the cardboard from her. "Cork, please," she wrote, though I had not told her where I wanted to go.

The accents bruised me, made me think of Colm.

When I got back to New York, I copied the names of all the health food stores on the north shore of Long Island and started a search. I found him in the produce aisle of a tiny organic market, with a cardboard box hoisted up on his shoulder and the same dent in his chin that always made me swoon like a heroine in a bad novel. He looked just as I remembered him but needed a shave.

We stood and appraised each other for a moment. Then we had a conversation of sorts, the automatic tossing out of phrases between people who haven't seen each other in a while. He implied that he and his wife had split, and after I paid for my groceries, he followed me outside.

"I've been to Ireland," I told him. I had not planned to mention this, had not wanted to reveal my extravagant, pitiful streak of romanticism.

"Have you now?" he shouted, rocking back on his heels. Traffic was racing by on the parkway; we had to shout to make ourselves heard.

I told him how I had hitchhiked around the perimeter of the country, how I was picked up by a milk truck driver who brought me to a pub in Ballyshannon. I was the only woman in the place, I said, then told how the bartender came out from behind the bar and insisted that I dance with him "We danced to 'Take Me Back to County Mayo,'" I said. I described the event in such a way that obliterated all the terror and menace.

"And you were out there all on your own, were you?" Colm said.

I said that I was.

"You're mad," he said, but not as if he meant it.

8

This year several of my friends got married all in a row. I have heard people claim that first marriages occur in chain reactions.

At wedding number one, a big Catholic society to-do in New Orleans, the maid of honor and two of the bridesmaids fainted. This was right in the middle of the ceremony. I hadn't been listening, but you can bet that got my attention. The first woman went down during the part of the service when the priest reads the passage from the Bible that goes, "Love is patient and kind; love is not jealous or boastful; it is not arrogant or rude. . . ." It's the passage everyone chooses for weddings. I've heard it so many times that all I can hear now when the priest reads it is "Love is always this, love is never that. . . ." We bridesmaids were kneeling on little wooden contraptions made especially for praying, and the bridesmaid on the end just keeled over, right onto the bride's long train. She yelped like a startled cat and then her body went limp.

Less than a minute later, the maid of honor collapsed, and she too was carried out to the foyer by a couple of guests who were doctors. After that the bride, who was in tears, kept glancing back at the seven remaining bridesmaids. The ones on either side of me had clasped my hands in theirs, so I could only nod to the bride. My friend Holly kept squeezing my hand and whispering, "I'm dizzy. I think I'm next."

"You're fine," I told her. I stopped listening to the ceremony and tried to make myself feel faint. I stared at the fuchsia sleeves of my taffeta dress until my eyes watered, but I felt solid as ever.

At the reception, everyone made a fuss over the bridesmaids. An elderly man in pince-nez and a bowler hat grabbed me under the elbows and propelled me toward the bar for a drink. He secured for me a generous glass of champagne. He then told me stories about fainting illnesses women had suffered in the eighteenth century. "Astonishing," he said, "that they're with us even today."

I said I'd noticed that the first bridesmaid who fainted seemed rather thin.

"A lovely girl," he said. "With a fine long neck, like a swan's."

9

I like to imagine I could be a different kind of woman, a more successful hybrid. That I could stay single by choice, support myself, vacation alone in places where I do not know the language, stride in an extravagant red dress through a concert hall. That I could stand on my sun-spangled patio each morning and whisper, "I love my life."

10

My friend Holly married an obstetrician. The most I can say for him is, at least he won't be squeamish in the delivery room when she has a baby. Of course, there will be babies. For now, sets of crystal and cutlery and tumblers. One of Holly's friends from high school gave her a bridal shower, and we discussed cutlery and tumblers on her screened-in porch, which was filled with white wicker and pillows and chintz. I thought about the words *cutlery* and *tumbler* and flipped through glossy magazines about dog breeding while Holly described some gifts she had received in the mail.

The day before the wedding, Holly had a bridesmaid's tea at the Stanhope Hotel in Manhattan. I borrowed an old silk dress from my mother and improvised with a safety pin at my waist.

We sat in chairs like couches around a low coffee table and were given menus with pictures of a Victorian woman's silhouette on them. The menu listed fifteen kinds of tea. A waiter in a white coat put strainers on all our cups and poured tea from a different silver teapot for each of us. Then he brought around finger sandwiches and we pointed to which ones we wanted and he placed them on our plates with tongs. There were salmon, cucumber, egg, watercress, and chicken, cut into squares and circles and triangles. The sandwiches were precisely the size that made eating them in two bites seem fussy but gluttonous in one. The mother-in-law of the bride ordered sherry for us, and we had scones and Devonshire cream with black currant, lemon, and raspberry jam in tiny pots. Then pastries filled with sweet fruit. The bride gave each of us bracelets in velvet boxes. My other friend, the New Orleans bride, turned over a plate and held it up while she fished in her purse for a pen to write down the name of the china pattern.

Holly put her seven bridesmaids in fuchsia, too. Now I have a pair of bright pink dresses hanging in my closet. Two giant, dusty valentines.

11

I visited Hinderly in Manhattan on what must have been the most humid night of this summer. We ate tiny portions of perfect, beautiful food at a restaurant with wobbly little tables set up right on the sidewalk. The car exhaust was so thick I could feel spools of it unraveling in my lungs. It didn't seem to bother Hinderly, who received thumps on the back from several men in suits and some quick pecks from women with shiny hair and powdered faces. Everyone gave me the eye, as if they knew something I didn't.

Back at his apartment, he made summery drinks, rum and pink fruit juice, with bright green wedges of lime.

"Please come upstairs with me," he said. He shimmied across the sofa and kissed me. His teeth grazed my lip.

His bedroom was air-conditioned. On one wall there was a framed poster commemorating an anniversary of the New York Stock Exchange.

"Just lie there with me," he said, pointing to his bed. "Just for a little bit."

You could look at the man and the woman in the air-conditioned room and see how arrangements could be made. It would be so easy, if love worked that way.

12

Colm and I planned to meet in the parking lot of the Country Squire, a restaurant halfway between our houses. I was staying at my parents' house during my summer holidays, and he was still living with his wife, though they slept in different rooms and had filed for a legal separation.

Driving to meet him, I began to worry that maybe he was going to hurt or even kill me. Maybe he secretly blamed me for the breakup of his marriage.

He was already there, waiting, in his van. I was deciding I would not under any circumstances get in that van when he got out and climbed into my car, just as he had when we worked at the health food store.

"Not parka weather, is it?" he said, kissing me full on the mouth.

We drove to a bar, and over pints of Guinness he told me about the two years of trying to make his marriage a livable arrangement. There had been plates thrown across rooms, threats by both of them to take their daughter and get on a plane back to Dublin, an incident in which his wife held a knife to his throat and cursed the day she met him.

I could not fathom how all this went on while I was teaching college freshmen to write coherent paragraphs and rushing around to weddings in fuchsia dresses.

There was more: "One day, her birthday, I went out to pick up a present for her, a leather coat I knew she wanted. While I was out, I ran into a friend and we went for a pint. When I got home, she was so angry at me for takin' the extra time, she took off her shoe and hit me with the heel of it until I was bleedin'. My chest was fuckin' bleedin'!"

"I can't imagine that at all," I said. The story struck me as comic and terrible.

We drove back to the Country Squire parking lot. We climbed into the backseat and I kissed him: face, ears, lips, neck. Then I lay back and listened to the wet, careful press of his mouth down my body.

I confessed that I had been worried he would hurt me.

He sat up and sighed. "Sarah," he said. "Do you not know me at all?"